Puffin Books

A DOG CALLED NELSON

There must be something different about a dog with one eye, something that can't be pinned down, not even by a tomcat . . .

Noggy and Bill are friends who live in the same street of a Lancashire mining town in the twenties. At the very centre of their lives is Nelson, the dog that Noggy's Uncle Gus left behind when he ran away to join the navy at the age of thirteen. With remarkable energy and rare insight, Bill recalls the ups and downs of Nelson's family's life, the scrapes he got them into and out of and the unique relationship between Nelson and his true master, Uncle Gus.

This thought-provoking and above all funny book will be enjoyed by anyone over ten.

Illustrated by Gavin Rowe

Bill Naughton

A Dog Called Nelson

Puffin Books

Puffin Books, Penguin Books Ltd, Harmondsworth, Middlesex, England
Penguin Books, 40 West 23rd Street, New York, New York 10010, U.S.A.
Penguin Books Australia Ltd, Ringwood, Victoria, Australia
Penguin Books Canada Ltd, 2801 John Street, Markham, Ontario, Canada L3R 1B4
Penguin Books (N.Z.) Ltd, 182–190 Wairau Road, Auckland 10, New Zealand

First published by J. M. Dent & Sons Ltd 1976
Published in Puffin Books 1984

Copyright © Bill Naughton, 1976
Illustrations copyright © Gavin Rowe, 1984
All rights reserved

Made and printed in Great Britain by
Richard Clay (The Chaucer Press) Ltd,
Bungay, Suffolk
Set in Monophoto Times

Contents

1. The secret of winning pigeon races

There was a lad used to live in the bottom end house in our street in Bolton when I was a boy who was known as Noggy. He had short red hair, little blue eyes, and he was on the small side. What he lacks in size, his mother used to say, he makes up for in cheek.

Noggy and I were good friends. We used to go around quite a bit together, and I was welcome at his house at any time. We had such a good understanding of one another you might even say we were chums, but we were not what you could call real good *mates*.

Now, although it may sound a bit daft to those who are not familiar with lads and their ways, the fact was, Noggy seemed always to be too busy to be a proper mate. I have never known one of these quick, spry, sharp, always-on-the-go sort of lads to make a good mate. They always seem to be away on their own. They'll never move at your speed – you've always got to move at theirs. Above all, they haven't time to listen. Words don't seem to make much impression on them. They are boys of action. Now for a real mate you don't necessarily need a good talker, for sometimes good talkers can turn out to be a bit one-sided, the same one talking all the time. But to be a real good mate a lad has got to be a good listener. A mate who hasn't time to listen to your troubles isn't much use. At least not to me. Noggy at heart was not much of a listener.

Besides, when I come to what I think is the very

interesting part of a story or happening – all about what I said to him and he said to me, and even more what I did to him and he did to me – at such spots I not only like to slow down the pace of our walking as we're going along the street, but at times I even like to stop. I might even put my hand on my mate's shoulder, and confide in him and tell him exactly what happened. Getting something off your chest with a mate you can trust seems to do you a lot of good. In fact I've only had one mate in all my life who answered all those needs. But that, I'm afraid, is another story.

Now that sort of thing, stopping and starting, was absolutely no use with Noggy. He would scarcely ever slow down, let alone stop. And, even if at times I got my mitt fastened on one of his elusive shoulders and faced him with an attitude of what I took to be that of the Ancient Mariner, half the time I was talking I could plainly see, in those small eyes of his, that he wasn't listening to me but thinking of what he was going to do next. Also he was full of remarks like: *Let's get a move on! We've got to buck up a bit! Let's get cracking! Away we go!* and one of his favourites, which was: *Don't let the conversation stop the job!* You can never get real matey with a chap like that.

Not that I blamed Noggy in any way for always being on the go, for when things have got to be done that's just the sort of person you need around. Talkers like myself are all right when you feel like a chat, but the world needs active people to keep things going. And Noggy had so much to do, what with chopping up firewood and selling it, feeding the donkey or pony, and above all, going off tossing the pigeons.

Jud, Noggy's dad, was a pigeon-fancier, and he had some of the best short-distance pigeons in that part of the world. It was Noggy's job, in the evenings and at

8

weekends, to take the pigeons to a certain mark up the Middle Brook and toss them up in the air.

I don't mean it quite like that, for you don't just toss pigeons into the air. When you go off tossing pigeons, you've got these pigeons in a closed basket. One with a lid on and a little stick you slide in place to see the lid doesn't open. You also need a stopwatch or chronometer. You get to a spot with maybe quarter of an hour to spare. Put the basket down and let the pigeons settle (you usually have two pigeons in the one basket with a wooden panel between them). Then a half-minute before the time you take one out, very gently, whispering to it all the time. Then at say ten seconds to spare you raise it aloft in your two hands and point it toward home. Then at five seconds to go you slowly draw your hand back with the pigeon in. Then dead on the second you gently but firmly send it forward, giving it confidence, and hoping it will rise slightly and make straight for home. All this has to be done to the split second, so I suppose Noggy got used to being concerned about time. I used to hold the clock and call out the seconds, *'Five – four – three – two – one – UP!'*

'Now listen,' Jud would say before we went off – I'll call him Jud because that was what Noggy called him – 'just listen –'

'I'm listenin',' Noggy would say. 'Carry on.'

Jud would make sure the watch or clock that Noggy took was synchronized to the very second with the watch or clock he kept at home to time the pigeon back. That is to say, if it was one minute and five seconds past seven on Noggy's timepiece it had to be exactly the same on Jud's. 'Ah tha listenin' too, Bill?' Jud would say.

'Aye, Bill's listenin' too,' Noggy would say, 'so let's get weavin' as soon as we can.'

'Right,' Jud would say, '– now listen. You'll be up at

9

the four-mile mark at say ten minutes to eight or near enough. Got me?'

'I've got you,' Noggy would say. 'Carry on.'

'Have you got me, too, Bill?' Jud would say.

'I've got you, too,' I would say, trying to get in first this time.

'Right,' Jud would say. 'Now that will give you a little rest – time for my pigeons to settle. But I don't want you to set 'em off at eight o'clock. Set the first off at exactly one minute past eight. Know why I said that?'

'Aye,' Noggy would say, 'in case somebody else is timin' our pigeons. You don't want 'em to know their speed. So's they'll think they're a minute slower than what they are.'

'Good,' says Noggy's Dad. 'Bill don't 'ave to understand that. But listen – keep your mouth shut. Don't say a word to anybody. I know they're all watchin' through their bedroom windows. In fact old Hardbattle has got his watch out an' is timin' them. One minute past eight. Then set the next off exactly two minutes later. Got me?'

'I've got you,' Noggy and I would say together.

'Right,' Jud would say. Then, before putting the pigeons in the basket, he would hold each pigeon with gentle firmness, up close to his mouth, and sort of coo to it.

Jud was not exactly what you could call a handsome man, for he had a big ugly broken nose, ferrety eyes, a cauliflower ear, and his mouth wasn't all that either, sort of large dewlaps. Also, he had a very rough grating voice, the sort of voice that would seem as though it could bring the rust off your bike frame. Of course, this was quite fitting to a man who was a hawker of firewood, and at times was a rag-tatter as well. When he yelled *Rag-a-bone* it was reckoned he could linger on the bone for a full minute if not longer, grating away like a faulty

foghorn, until the very air in the backstreet was set off
vibrating, and shirts and bloomers and one thing and
another on the clothes-line would all start a-shaking.
You would swear that in place of tonsils he had a little
emery wheel or sandpaper stuck in his gullet. But it used
to bring the customers out with their old rags. Anything
to shut him up.

Oh, but it was so different when he cooed to his pigeons
– for then an amazing change took place. The first time I
heard him I could hardly believe my own ears. His voice
came out that soft and mellifluous it would have charmed
a sparrow down from the housetops. 'My little beauty,'

he whispered, his big nose nuzzling up against the pigeon, '– you'll show 'em how to fly. Ee, but you're bonny . . . you're the bonniest bird I've ever 'ad in my 'ole life!'

Looking at the pigeon's eyes, and there's not really all that to see in a pigeon's eyes, you'd swear that bird understood every single word. And the odd thing was, suddenly this great ugly mug of Jud's became gentle, and whilst I couldn't have said he was goodlooking, he became not so unattractive. One time he must have seen I was watching him, for when he had put the pigeon down he turned to me and said: 'Know what the secret is, Billy – that I win all my pigeon races with?'

My ears went back like a shot. Jud was a famous pigeon-flyer and breeder, and the other flyers were always after secrets such as diet and one thing and another for the reason of his success.

'No . . .' I said. 'What?'

He stooped down and whispered one word in my ear. I couldn't believe it. I looked up at him, at his piggy eyes that seemed suddenly to have enlarged, and were smiling softly as it were, on me, and I pretended I hadn't heard.

'What was that?' I said.

He put his hefty dewlaps together once more and I listened hard and I heard him sort of coo into my ear: *'Love!'*

'Love!' I said, and I felt baffled beyond belief, '– love makes pigeons win races?'

'Love,' said Jud, 'makes the world go round. So why shouldn't it make pigeons win races? Listen,' he went on, 'they used to say of me when I was a lad,' and his expression became serious, even a little sad, so I thought, 'that I wasn't too bright in the top storey.' And to emphasize the point he tapped the side of his head. Looking at him, as he sort of gawped at me to allow me time for his words to sink in, the thought struck me that it was easy to believe he was telling the truth. He did not exactly look all there.

'I was more than 'opeless at school,' he went on. 'Every day was mortal agony to me. 'istory ... King 'enry the Eighth tellin' the sea to go back – William the Conqueror burnin' them cakes – an' whatsaname wi' the whatsaname – it was all some 'orrible nightmare to me. They all sounded off their 'eads to me. I never believed a word of it. I didn't know why I was there in school. I couldn't reckon up the simplest sum. In fact I didn't see the point of pounds, shillings an' pence unless the money was real. So's nearly every day I used to play wag, an' go off to the stables where my Uncle Charlie was horsekeeper. I could get on better wi' 'orses an' dogs an' other animals than I could with sums an' history. These were real. The others were all in the head. One day Uncle Charlie caught me shouting at a horse to move over. "Jud," he said, "never frighten an animal. Always speak gently to 'em. A frightened animal is a dangerous animal. Think on what I'm tellin' you," he said, "always be firm – but be fair. An' love 'em – an' in that way you'll win their trust. Always have your animal trust you – so that it is sure you will never do it no harm. Then, as the animal learns from you, you will learn from the animal."' Jud thought back: 'They were good words.'

'But where does love come in with pigeons?' I asked.

'For a start,' said Jud, 'I love all my pigeons an' they love me. Love makes people 'appy an' it makes birds 'appy. When birds are 'appy they are like people – they start lovin' each other. Now, when I fly this lovely little cock pigeon, Egbert, next Sunday – he'll fly 'ome like mad to be back with his mate, Queenie, an' their 'appy little family. An' she's the same. An' they don't light on the gutter up there like so many pigeons do – they land on the let-board in the loft there. They can't bear to be

13

separated. An' the let-board on the loft is the winnin' post – not the ledging up there. Ooh an' they don't 'alf welcome each other. Love, see. Love is a wonderful thing – it makes the world go round.' Then Jud put his hand into his trouser-pocket and jingled what sounded like silver, and added: 'And over the years it has won me a lot of money. Love is a wunnerful thing.'

2. They say one volunteer is worth two pressed men

Jud was not Noggy's real father. He was his stepfather. Why I haven't gone on about it or even mentioned it up to this, is because Noggy himself never bothered about it. It all seemed very natural to him. Once, at the street-corner, one of the lads – a lad called Pongo, not a bad sort but a bit of a bighead – brought it up about what a pity it was Noggy had only a stepfather whilst all of us had what he called real fathers, but Noggy would have none of his sympathy.

'One volunteer,' said Noggy, 'is worth two pressed men.'

This was a wartime saying of the period, which meant of course that one soldier who went voluntarily to war was worth two of those who were conscripted and compelled to join up.

'How do you mean?' said Pongo.

'Well, when you were born,' said Noggy, looking at old Pongo with a very close and critical eye, 'your dad had to take what came. He had to father you whether he liked you or not. He had no choice. But Jud saw me beforehand, and knew what he was taking on. I respect him all the more for it. An' I even respect myself the more for it, too.'

It seems that Noggy's father, Ernest Nogg, had been Jud's mate. They were born next door to each other, they played as children together, went to school together, and they had joined up together in the Great War that broke out on 4 August 1914 between the Allies and Germany.

Ernest and Jud had been lucky, and apart from a wound or two had survived until the big German offensive that took place in the spring of 1918. Ernest got killed by a sniper's bullet. Sorry for going into details but I want to make the picture clear. Ernest was married and they had three small children – Noggy being the eldest. Then when the Armistice was declared at 11 a.m. on 11 November 1918, and the war was over, Jud was demobilized shortly after – they called it *demobbed* – and he came home and straightaway went round and asked Noggy's mother to marry him.

In fact I did once hear that he had actually proposed in a letter from the trenches some months after Ernest's death. But Ranee – that was Mrs Nogg's first name – had turned him down. Jud's idea was that he couldn't go and marry some single girl when his best mate's widow was there with three youngsters to bring up. Also, it seems that Jud had promised Ernest that if he, Ernest, got killed, and he, Jud, came through, he would marry Ranee and see the three young children had a father. And it wasn't merely a father, but a father that wasn't a stranger. They lived very close in those days. I should perhaps explain that it was the sort of arrangement men came to at the time, for life was more of a struggle. A home with young children needed a man around to keep it afloat.

But it seems that when Jud went round and proposed in person, explaining that, although he personally was not the marrying sort, and preferred to go around with all his troubles under his cap, he and Ernest had been like blood brothers, and that it was only right he should now marry Ranee, she turned him down flat.

'I'm a woman,' she said, 'and I don't want marrying out of pity. If I marry at all I want to marry out of love.'

'But I don't love you,' said Jud. 'I never have. An' I doubt if I ever will.'

'I don't love you either,' said Ranee. 'In fact I don't even *like* you. And further, I never have liked you. I only used to put up with you coming round in the old days because you were Ernest's pal. So there!'

So then Jud looked round the house, looked at Noggy and the two younger ones who were all playing dominoes, and said: 'Well, Ranee, now we understand each other it'll not be as though we were going into it with our eyes shut. An' I did promise old Ernest faithfully.'

So Ranee looked Jud up and down and said: 'Well, I can't see any Prince Charming coming along in your place. So if it's all right by you, Jud, I don't see why it shouldn't be all right by me. Especially as you were Ernest's pal.' And so once the air was cleared, what do Jud and Ranee do but go and get married. Perhaps it wasn't all that romantic – I don't know – but as marriages go it was not a bad little marriage.

I'm not sure why I'm telling all this, except I want to give a good picture of the family and the times so that the story that is coming will be fully understood. And another thing . . . in the main, the story is more about another character, two others in fact, not yet even mentioned!

Anyway, as I say, it was quite a happy little marriage in its way. Twelve months after the wedding day Ranee was confined, as they used to put it, and she gave birth to triplets, two boys and a girl. It gave Jud a bit of a shock.

'About a year ago,' I once heard him say, 'I wrote to Blackpool for digs for the holiday week and it was for me – I was a happy young bachelor, d'you see, everything I asked for was for one – now it's for *eight*! Eight – it's a bit of a jump up I can tell you – in a year. Especially for a chap used to having all his troubles under his cap.' Jud went on about all this when I was sitting there – I prefer those families that don't always try to hide things from the children – and I remember Ranee saying: 'Has it ever struck you how lucky you were compared to most men – to come right into a readymade family? Think of the trouble you've saved yourself.'

They were a very easygoing family, no fuss or bother, and I'll tell of one little incident to show what I mean. They had this large backyard, a sort of long one, with a little stable at the bottom. People had stables all over the place in those days, there were so many horses and ponies about, mostly for hawkers and street traders and the

18

like. Also, they used this backyard for chopping up firewood which would be sold at a halfpenny or twopence a
bucketful.

Very often I'd be round there giving a hand and
Noggy's mother would make us all tea which we could
have there in the backyard. Now, one time there were no
chairs or boxes for the triplets to sit on – they must have
been around three at the time – and Jud said: 'Don't
worry – I'll get Sylvia.'

Sylvia was a gentle old donkey he had for pulling the
small firewood cart, although he had Tom, a light pony,
for the heavier work. So Jud brought Sylvia up to the
table and very gently said: 'Down . . . down, old girl.'
And Sylvia sort of went down on her knees. Donkeys
have a funny way of going down on their knees, as if
they were used to it. So then he sat the three of them on
Sylvia's back, just as though it were a bench. Old Sylvia
didn't mind, so long as she kept getting pieces of bread
and jam passed to her. In fact, she got so used to it all
that the moment Ranee appeared with that teapot she'd
go down on her own beside the table. Sometimes one of

the youngsters would forget and lean backwards and tumble off. But none of them ever got hurt, and it was always good for a laugh.

Now, I am not saying there was anything special or extraordinary about having a donkey for a seat, but let's say that it is a bit unusual. However, the family took no notice of it. If royalty had been present they would have done just the same. They never showed off and were very open.

Ranee, Noggy's mother, was a small dainty woman. She had been born in India, where her father was a sergeant in the army, and that was how she had got her name Ranee, which is Hindoo for queen. Although small she was a terrific chopper of firewood, and she would use an axe that was almost as sharp as a razor. She was a cricketer too – a tremendous batter. It seems they were out in the wilds in India most of the time and she and her brothers spent most days playing cricket.

She used to cut Noggy's hair with him on a stool out in the backyard. She had a pair of fournoughts clippers – they cut the closest you can get to the scalp – and a pudding basin which she would put over Noggy's head and run the clippers up to the edge. In this way you got an even line, but I wouldn't say it looked all that smart when finished. Not what you would called *styled*. I remember one occasion she cut my hair. Unfortunately, the pudding basin wouldn't fit over my head, and her mind must have been taken off the job so often, what with the triplets and one thing and another, that she made a right mess of it. I was lucky enough, however, to catch measles the same evening – Noggy said I must have brought the illness on out of misery – so that I had a fortnight at home, during which time my hair grew enough to cover up the disaster.

3. Nelson amongst the chaps at the streetcorner

Although I have told of Jud and Ranee, and Noggy and the family generally, I haven't yet mentioned the one character that helped to keep things running smoothly in and around that home. This was the dog Nelson.

You might wonder how a dog can help run a home, and so I'll tell you. Jud kept his pigeons and Ranee liked her cats – they always had at least three cats. Now, if there's one thing pigeons don't go mad about having around it's cats. And most cats enjoy having a go at a pigeon. It's in their nature. So when they got married and Jud arrived with his pigeons – one of the first things he got was a pair – there was the question as to whether the cats should go or the pigeons. And Ranee gave Jud to understand that if the cats went she would go, too. At the same time she was an understanding woman and saw that the pigeons brought out a certain tenderness in Jud. She knew that if you frustrate a man, those good feelings that are shut off have a way of turning nasty. And I suppose it is the same with a woman. There used to be a saying in the street amongst mothers: Never go too much against a child's nature – or it'll come out some other way. It was the same with these fathers who happened to have a son who was on the timid side, and they would constantly train the boy to be aggressive. If you don't bash him, they would say, I'll bash you. Watch out, the old women would say, you'll be the first to suffer. And it often happened that way – that a onetime timid son would turn on his father.

Just the same, the cats and the pigeons did look like a problem. But Nelson solved that problem more or less on the first day. The cats naturally put an eye on the pigeons at once. And I might say it wasn't a friendly eye. The pigeons became nervous and wouldn't eat. Something had to be done. So old Nelson let the cats wander around as usual, excepting when they put a foot within the area of the pigeon cotes. Then he would let out such a low threatening growl the cats would be off. Not that he scared the cats too much, for what with the little stable and one thing and another there was a tendency for rats and mice to appear, if you didn't have cats around. Of course if Nelson spotted a rat that was the end of the rat. One leap and he would have that rat by

the neck, and one sharp twist of his head and that neck was broken.

By the way, if ever the rats threatened to get out of hand, and they do breed very fast, Jud used to bring out the ferret called Freddy. He was really kept for when Jud was going after rabbits. You feed ferrets mostly on milk, and they have to be kept warm, so Jud would take him everywhere inside his shirt. Yes, he would open his shirt front and pop Freddy in next to his bare skin. Ever seen a ferret's teeth? – why, they're as sharp as sharp. You'd never have got me to do that with a ferret. But Freddy would never bite Jud – although anyone else was fair game. Jud would put Freddy down a rathole – sleek things ferrets – and in no time you got the rats flying out. Not a one would ever escape with Nelson around.

It wasn't just keeping the cats and pigeons in order and the rats down that Nelson was good at, but it was with the family as well. In fact he was just like one of the

family – a sort of superior member. One of the problems of a big family was getting them all in for their meals, because they'd start playing games and forget the time.

'Nelson, where's Edith?' Ranee would say. 'Go off an' find our Edith – tea's ready.'

Nelson would be off like a shot down the bottom of the street where the girls gathered and played their games, and in a tick he would be up to Edith, giving her the warning and pushing or pulling her home if she resisted. It was the same with the rest of the family. He knew everybody's name – he had a marvellous memory for names – and Ranee or Jud had only to say the word and he would be after any one of them. And if they weren't playing he went around until he found them, sniffing at front doors, for he knew all their friends. Also, Nelson was the one who would waken them up for school in the morning. First Ranee would put her head round the bottom of the stairs and beat on the wooden panel and call them, but often they didn't answer. Then she had only to whisper to Nelson and he would shoot upstairs and leap on to the bed. This would set the girls off laughing and they would rise in a good temper.

And another duty he was quite good at was being on what they called *bailiff guard*. There were some chaps going around in those days – and for all I know there might be still a few going around today – commonly known as *bum bailiffs* or just *bums*. The way it happened was like this: if someone had bought something from a shop on what was known as the *never*, that is, paying instalments of so much a week – it very often happened when times were good – then they might find themselves out of work. They would get in arrears with their payments. Then the owners of the shop – they would not be local men as a rule – would have a Court Order made against you to recover the goods and also further costs.

24

To carry out this order they employed these bailiffs, usually rather big men, perhaps retired policemen or the like, or say a man who had been a redcap, that is a *military* policeman. It had to be someone trained to use authority. They would call on the house and attempt to gain entry. They were not allowed to break the door in, but they could rush in if someone left it open.

Now, oddly enough, these chaps for the most part were very nice simple men – not ruffians or the like. Having gained entry they would sit down and state the amount of money required – perhaps two or three pounds. If that was not forthcoming they would be allowed by law to take that amount in furniture. The woman would usually have a cry if they got in, beg them not to take things, ask them not to let her husband know, perhaps even swear at them, then she would make them a pot of tea. The bailiffs didn't want to take any furniture, for the truth was, the entire furniture of most homes would not bring a couple of pounds in most markets. So they would hang on to get what money they could for those who employed them. And mostly they said they were personally very sorry.

Once or twice Jud and Ranee had somehow got in debt and were afraid the bailiffs might get in, so they used to set Nelson on bailiff guard: 'Watch for the bums, Nelson,' she would say, 'and if they attempt to get in, you give it 'em.'

At the very mention of the word *bums* old Nelson would start growling, baring his teeth, and generally trying to turn himself into a bull terrier. And heaven help any who tried to get in. They weren't going to have any of their furniture, Court Order or not – not if Nelson could help it. That's the nice thing about families who get into trouble – they stick together. Down to the dog.

Another thing about Nelson – although I don't want to go on praising him, but I must be fair – he was a wonderful house minder and child minder, when Ranee and Jud went out anywhere. Above all, he had a tender heart, and if a row broke out, which seems likely enough in any family, Nelson would go at once to the one who was upset, perhaps crying, and start licking his or her face, and generally making a fuss. It's surprising how a thing like that, an animal showing a concern and understanding, can affect people.

'Stop rowing,' Noggy would say, 'you're upsetting Nelson.' A funny thing, but a man and woman who

might say hard things to each other would seem to quieten down when the dog got upset.

But what Nelson seemed to enjoy most of all was coming along to the streetcorner for an hour in the evenings with Noggy and settling in amongst the lads there. I won't go into detail describing Nelson since you can form your own picture of him when I tell you that, on his mother's side, he was a cross between a Welsh sheepdog and an Irish spaniel. On the father's side he was a cross between a Scottie and a Boston terrier (these would be his grandparents, so to speak, if you follow me). And there was a trace of French poodle, which may have given him his occasional touch of uppishness, and Jud reckoned he must have some whippet in him, the speed he could move. So you might say he was a bit of a mixture. Oh, and before I forget, he had the eyes of a Labrador. Or should I say *the eye* of a Labrador, for Nelson had only one eye, that being the reason for his name. But that one eye, although at times it looked sad, in the way a Labrador sometimes looks sad, was as sharp and as cunning as could be. However, if he put that eye on you for anything he wanted, you would need a heart of stone to refuse him.

Nelson's one fault, if you could call it that, was that he was inclined to be a bit too matey amongst the lads. The minute we started playing a game he wanted to join in. In fact he was quite useful at cricket, for he never minded mugging after the ball for you, and this saved your legs a bit. So we would set him at longstop and on the boundary. At football he was a dab hand, or perhaps I mean a *dab nose*, for he was an expert at balancing a ball. Of course, the most we ever put up with him would be the first five minutes, and then he would get sent off.

Another time he could get a bit too matey was when we were all gathered there at the streetcorner, squatting down on our hunkers, as they used to say, in imitation of the coalminers at the Men's Corner. Nelson had a way of worming in amongst us, resting his chin on your shoulder, and listening to the tales that were being told. Sometimes, one of the lads would take another lad's cap off and stick it on Nelson's head and then he did look a rum sight. In fact Nelson often struck me as being a dog who in his heart really longed to be a lad, but since things hadn't turned out that way he was making the best of a bad job. And so, with the cap over his blind eye, and the other eye sort of gleaming with excitement, he would listen to the tale that was being told, with the lads talking to him as though he were one of them: 'Take your blinkin' big head off my shoulders willya!' or 'Keep your rotten tail out of my eyes if you don't mind!' Nelson tended to forget himself when a tale was being told, and when it came to the end he would open his mouth as though laughing, although no sound would come out for quite a time, and then there would be a sort of hoarse chuckle. You know how it is when somebody has a funny laugh – it seems to set off all the others, and that was what used to happen when Nelson laughed. A funny dog Nelson.

Pongo and Noggy and one or two others reckoned that Nelson knew every word of every tale, but they would never get me to believe that, although I must admit there was one tale, Nelson's favourite, over which he would always be the first to burst out laughing. Not that it was a very good tale, but somehow it tickled him. It was called 'The Three Tramps in the Oven', and although it's on the gruesome side I suppose I can tell it, since after all it is only a tale.

There was this Waddilove's bakery, near the canal it was, and they reckoned that one cold morning Mr Waddilove went in and opened the huge oven door and what

28

does he find but three men, three tramps, who have all crept into this big oven to have a night's kip in the warmth, and what do they do but suffocate – so Mr Waddilove had these three dead bodies. He didn't want to call the police because that might have turned folk against his bread. But there was this chap called Ambrose who worked for him, who wasn't quite right in the head, and so he took out one of the bodies and said to Ambrose: 'Hy, can you get rid of this chap for me – he slept in the oven and he's a goner?' So Ambrose said: 'Sure, I'll put him in a sack an' fling him into the deep end of the canal. Leave it to me.'

So Ambrose did just that and watched the body sink. But when he came back Mr Waddilove had got another body out and he said: 'Hy, that chap you've supposed to have got rid of – he musta got out of the sack – he's back again.' 'Get off,' said Ambrose. 'This time,' he said, 'I'll put some bricks in the sack as well.' So he put some bricks in the sack along with the second body, and went and flung the sack in the canal.

When he got back to the bakery old Waddilove had the third body ready. 'Ambrose, he's back again – before you.' 'Boss, leave it to me,' said Ambrose, 'I'll fix him.' So this time he put some iron in the sack, and just to make sure he got an axe and chopped one of the legs off the body. And he tied the sack up tight. And he heaved it into the deepest part of the canal. And he watched it go down. And he waited but there was no movement. And he stood there until it came on raining heavily. Then he went back up toward the bakery. (Now this was the part where old Nelson used to start gurgling, ready for the laugh.)

As Ambrose got up near the bakery there chanced to be a one-legged fellow coming along who was all wet through from the rain. And when he saw Ambrose he said: 'What weather! Hy, is this Waddilove's bakery?' And Ambrose stared at this one-legged chap, all wet with rain, and he got very suspicious, and he said: 'What do you want at Waddilove's bakery?' And the one-legged chap said: 'I'm going to see Mr Waddilove –' And Ambrose said: 'You are hell as like! I've had enough trouble with you – escaped three times. Don't think I don't know who you are with that one leg. I'll tell you where you're going – you're goin' back in that flamin' canal where you just come from!' And he picked up the poor one-legged chap on his shoulder and carried him kicking and struggling to the canal and flung him in.

Not a very good tale, but it does give some idea of the sort of streetcorner tale going round at the time. For some reason old Nelson found the idea of an innocent one-legged man getting flung in the canal quite hilarious, and first you'd get this silent snigger followed by a hoarse raspy chuckle, which set all the lads off laughing. In fact, that was the only reason the tale got told for we'd hear it until it was threadbare, but Nelson couldn't hear it often enough. Just the same, I refuse to believe he understood it, although all the others reckoned he did. He certainly knew the gory bits.

4. Walk in backwards and pretend to be coming out

One of the things to get into each week, so far as we lads were concerned, was the First House at the Derby Picture Palace on a Monday evening. One reason for this was that then you were in demand to tell the others what was on, and was it worth going to see. Of course you never admitted to it being a rotten show, because most of the lads like to boast. Also, if you had been done you wanted someone else to be done as well.

A visit to the pictures in those days was different from today. For a start there were two houses – that is to say, the First House emptied and the Second House came in. This meant they could take more money at the box office. Also, you were never interrupted during a film with people coming and going.

It was often very hard to raise the twopence needed to go to the First House, and there was a great deal of what was known as *pinching in*. Now the way to go about that was to *walk in backwards and pretend you were going out*. That is to say, if you had no money, you would hang around outside the big *exit* doors until the First House was over and you heard the bolts being drawn and the doors opening.

As the doors opened the rush of patrons would issue forth, their faces flushed and their eyes often red. Those early films flickered so much that you could not watch long without your eyes showing the strain. That was your moment for sneaking in. But it was no use going in

31

facing the mob coming out, for you'd get swept backwards and off your feet. So what you had to do was turn your back on the mob and force your way backwards inside the cinema. If anybody said anything to you: 'Out the flamin' way,' or anything of that sort, you simply said: 'Sorry – but I've forgotten my cap.' That was sort of making out you had already been inside.

Getting inside was only half the battle, for they wouldn't let the new customers in at the paybox until they were sure, or thought they were sure, that everybody was outside. But the smell of the inside of the Derby Picture Palace, which was a musty mixture of films, people, tobacco smoke and orange peel, would so excite a lad that he would do almost anything rather than be turned out. You could hide under the seats, or sneak up behind the piano, or dodge under a curtain or slip into the toilets and climb on top and lie down on top of a lavatory, so that no one could see you, and then quietly move into a seat once the Second House patrons had begun to move in. It wasn't easy. But it was very exciting.

Nelson was not one to be left out of the fun and, no matter what watch was placed on the doors, Nelson would find his way in. The owner of the Derby Picture Palace in those days was a man called Tutty Booth. He was quite a nice chap, really, with wavy ginger hair. Everybody to do with pictures seemed to have wavy hair, for the crippled woman in the paybox had wavy hair, and so had the operator. But Tutty Booth could not stand old Nelson. The reason was simple. We boys went in the *Tuppennies*. They were not individual seats, of course, but just rows of wooden benches. And you had bare wooden boards under your feet. As soon as the lights went down old Nelson would find his way in and come straight to us in the dark. He liked sitting on my

lap, but he was a bit of a weight, and we used to spread him out a bit between two or three of us.

Nelson enjoyed Charlie Chaplin comedies, and especially all the kicking up the backside that went on in them. But his favourite films were what are now called *Westerns*, but were then known as *Cowboy films*. What he couldn't stand were *society dramas*, films all about toffs, in which the men wore evening dress most of the time and looked right cissies, and the women had long gowns and lots of necklaces, and they sort of gaped at one another making out they were in love. Anything to do with what they called *love* used to bore old Nelson stiff. You could tell almost from the start when a film was going to be no good, but it seemed the audience would hang on, hoping for something to happen.

It was an understood thing amongst us lads that any mate who had got up early, say a little-piecer in the mill or a lad who went round with papers and had to be up about half past five every morning, could work in a little kip. He would rest his head down on the back of the

33

wooden seat in front of him, or even on someone's lap. 'Wakken me up when something happens,' he would say, '– or when this is over an' the comic starts.' As soon as old Nelson spotted this he would join in, for he just couldn't stand the actors looking ga-ga at one another, and he would look round for a handy shoulder, arm or knee to get his head down on, and at the same time he would let out one of those long loud yawns that some dogs are very good at. If the yawn didn't set the audience off, very soon his snores would. As Pongo used to say, they didn't sound like dog snores but more like some prehistoric animal frightening off all intruders.

The films were silent of course, except for this grating buzz from the projection box, and it seemed that Nelson would wait until the woman who played the piano had stopped to rest her fingers for a few moments. She used to play 'In a Monastery Garden' for religious scenes, and if there was a chase with horses she would play a galloping march, and in time her fingers seemed to get cramp or something, and she would stop playing and rub them. It would be just that moment of silence when Nelson would let out one or two of his loudest snores, and follow up quickly with some long, weird, whining moans, that sounded as though they might be coming from a dog stranded on some wild, lonely shore, and threatened with a slow, lingering death from sheer boredom.

Any trickle of interest the film may have had would be slashed stone dead at the sound of that great snoring moan from Nelson. Folk could hear it away back in the posh tanner seats. Then somebody would laugh. And that would set the lot off. Then the youngsters in their clogs would start stamping on the wooden floor and at the same time yelling out: 'Take it off, Tutty! Take it off!' What with the stamping and yelling the place would be in an uproar, and the film would have to stop and the

34

lights come on. Tutty Booth would attempt to address the audience from the stage but no one would listen: 'Send for a cowboy film!' they would yell. 'We're not paying good money to watch that sort of stuff.' Then someone would shout: 'Why, even the dog went to sleep!' So what would happen then would be that the boring film would be taken off, a short comic film put on, until Tutty Booth had borrowed a film from another cinema. 'If only I could find that dog,' he used to say. 'They would never have known but for him.'

5. Nelson makes a dazzling stage appearance

Another place that Noggy and I used to get to, sometimes with Pongo, was the Grand Theatre, in Churchgate, Bolton. This was what they called a variety theatre, where you might get a number of turns from comedians to contortionists, and acrobats to singers, and nearly always a chorus of what looked to me very glamorous young women, who would dance in a row at the footlights, kicking their lovely legs high into the air.

You went up a lot of narrow stairs, into what they called the gods, the price of a seat was fourpence. You seemed to be so far away when you went in that the stage was hardly visible, but once the house lights went down and the footlights came on you could see fairly well. I loved going there. And so did old Nelson, but he had been definitely barred by the doorkeeper. He had sneaked past the chap once or twice, but now when he saw us – a little chap he was, and very awkward – he always looked for Nelson.

Anyway, on this particular evening, Noggy, Pongo and myself had earned ourselves sixpence each from chopping firewood all day and had decided to go to the Grand. Of course we had to keep it secret from old Nelson, not even talk about it in front of him, and when we did even mention it we would avoid saying the actual word, and simply spell it out: 'G-r-a-n-d.' That dog was so artful he would know at once. And even then you would see that he suspected something, the way he went about and watched us. He knew we were up to something, but what it was he could only suspect.

About six o'clock, just before we had arranged to go, Jud sent Nelson to find one of the triplets, and whilst he was away on that errand we slipped quietly off.

We got nicely away without being spotted, and we were making our way down Derby Street, giving the odd look behind just to make sure we weren't being followed, and generally feeling pretty pleased with ourselves, when Pongo suddenly stopped.

'Hy, chaps,' he said, 'look ahead there – at John Street corner. Can you spot anything?' Then he added: 'Somethin' keeps showin' an' then disappearin'.'

'What d'you mean,' said Noggy, who, as I have said, couldn't bear being held up in any way, '– keeps showin' an' then disappearin'?'

'Exactly what I said,' said Pongo. 'You look straight ahead at that bit of the front of the pub. Nothin' there now – but just stop an' watch it.'

We all looked, and at first I couldn't see anything. The next thing I saw something just tip itself out.

'If I'm not mistaken,' said Pongo, 'that's old Nelson's nose.' The next moment Pongo was proved right, for what was unmistakably Nelson's head and the one gleaming eye revealed itself.

'The rotten cunnin' cur,' said Noggy. 'He's been ahead all the time – watchin' us when we thought we were watchin' him.'

Once he knew he had been spotted Nelson showed his face. Noggy went up to him and gave him a terrible telling off there in the street in front of everybody. Nelson never liked anything of that sort, he was a very sensitive dog, and he looked at me, but I couldn't say anything. So he went off. He didn't slink off, he just went off. Nelson wasn't one to put his tail between his legs.

'I don't think you should've gone on at him like that,' I said.

'I had to get rid of him,' said Noggy.

'You hurt his feelings,' said Pongo.

'I don't trust him – that he's gone 'ome,' said Noggy.

And sure enough, some five minutes later Pongo stopped us again as we were at the Town Hall Square. 'Look,' he said, 'there's somethin' peepin' out from behind one of the lions.' Nelson disappeared and it was the same again a bit farther ahead, he was watching out for us at the corner of Mealhouse Lane. That dog knew every step you were going to take before you took it.

Anyway, when we got outside the Grand Theatre there was a sad parting. The awkward little doorkeeper spotted Nelson and he darted inside for a big walking-stick – he was a slight cripple as well – and when he came out he put the walking-stick to his shoulder as though it was a gun and pretended firing at Nelson. Actually, now I come to think of it, I suppose he was not a bad little chap at heart, and only put this fierce manner on to help get through the day. Old Nelson was not kidded of course – you wouldn't get him mistaking a walking-stick for a gun. Just the same, he could see he wasn't wanted and he went off round the corner looking rather unhappy.

'Noggy,' I said, 'won't he get lost?'

'Him – lost!' said Noggy. 'Not likely. He once found his way home through Manchester.'

'He might get run over,' said Pongo.

'Aye,' I said, 'perhaps we should see him home.'

'Listen,' said Noggy, 'when he comes to cross a road he not only looks both ways, but he even looks upwards to see there's nothin' comin' down. He'll be all right. In fact, I shouldn't be at all surprised if he doesn't hang about till we come out. Come on, chaps – let's get moving!'

So we went in to the Grand Theatre. I had Nelson on my mind, but it seemed once the chorus girls started dancing I began to forget him. 'Haven't they got lovely legs,' I said. 'Get off,' said Pongo, 'they're all bloomin' old women.' Pongo did have sharp eyes. After he said that I found I kept thinking of old Nelson. He was one of those dogs that had a way of getting into your thoughts when he wasn't there. I mean perhaps it was that one eye of his that seemed to hypnotize you, so that his image kept coming back.

It was after the interval that the top-of-the-bill act came on. And in a way I forgot old Nelson then. It was called 'Blondo and his Famous Performing Canines'. And what wonderful dogs they were, those performing canines. They seemed to be all of one breed, sort of poodles or getting on that way, and after they had done most of their turns this Blondo brought on a ball, and he got a ball match going between them, with goals on the stage.

40

I must say the audience enjoyed that act, seeing all these lovely poodle dogs heading the ball to one another. Then suddenly Pongo turned and whispered: 'Hy, lads – can you see anything sticking out down there near the side of the stage?'

That chap Pongo had eyes like a hawk. Above all, it seemed he was always looking at some spots where no one else was looking. If ever you went a walk with him he would always end up with a coin or two he had spotted in the gutter.

'What're you talkin' about?' said Noggy, looking rather annoyed.

'See what?' I said.

'Down in that left-hand corner,' he said, 'just behind that bit of scenery jutting out. Can't you see something?'

'Can't we see what?' said Noggy. 'Are you off again?'

'It looks like old Nelson's nose,' said Pongo. 'Just like it. An' a bit of that eye of his.'

'Don't talk daft,' said Noggy.

And just at that moment, when the football and heading game was going on between all those lovely trained dogs, all beautifully cared for, there was a sort of joyous yelp – that was certainly Nelson's – and the next thing old Nelson made his entrance. He came scuttering on to that brightly-lit stage, gave a saucy look at the audience – the other dogs never looked across the footlights – and then he went in amongst those performing dogs – and boy, did he show them how to play football!

Of course, those poor dogs didn't know what had happened and they were thrown into some confusion. And as for Blondo himself – a magnificent figure of a man he was – well, it was as though he was seeing things and couldn't believe his own eyes. As for myself, I must admit that for one whole minute, or maybe not a full minute, perhaps only ten seconds, but it felt a lot longer,

I went dry in the throat and seemed to stop breathing, and couldn't speak – I mean there were so many different feelings going on inside me. And I think it was the same with Noggy and, to some extent, Pongo – although he had sort of warned us.

I had this feeling we would all get in trouble for a start, and then I thought these dogs might all set about Nelson – and it also seemed certain that Nelson was going to ruin the show. But as I say, whatever my feelings were, they were nothing to what Blondo's feelings seemed to be. There he was, all dressed up as a sort of circus master, surrounded by his dogs, and suddenly old one-eyed Nelson had turned up in the middle of the act. I looked at Noggy. His eyes were almost out of his head with amazement. But he put his finger to his lips: '*Sh . . . sh . . . sh . . . sh . . .*' he whispered, '– *don't let on!*'

Whatever we felt, or Blondo himself felt, or his famous trained dogs, there was no doubt what the audience felt. They started laughing and cheering and clapping as old Nelson dribbled that ball about with his nose, headed it in the air, and went through both goals with it – to show how easy it was – and had these famous dogs mystified.

The audience had only clapped before Nelson appeared, now they were clapping and laughing, and it seemed the entire atmosphere changed.

Then, as the patrons up in the gallery joined in the laughter and applause, Pongo turned to Noggy and me and whispered: 'They think it's all part of the act.'

It would take somebody like Pongo to cotton on to that fact. It would certainly never have occurred to me.

'How do you mean?' said Noggy.

'The audience,' said Pongo, 'don't know it's your dog Nelson. How would they? They think it's one of Blondo's dogs. The comedian of the show, see – brought on late to bring some life to the act. It's called buildin' up, see.'

'What?' said Noggy.

'All the audience,' said Pongo, 'don't know it's your Nelson. They think it's Blondo's dog – brought on to make some fun!'

Just as we realized this, it seemed that Blondo himself, not a dullwitted fellow, grasped on to it too, and he flung Nelson a sweet, and tried to get his own dogs to join in more, and he began to bow to the torrents of applause.

Noggy then put his thumb and forefinger in his mouth and gave a whistle. As soon as Nelson heard that he stopped dead – balancing the ball on his head. The whole theatre went quiet. Then Nelson dropped the ball. He came to the front of the stage and looked upward. The audience burst into further cheering. Then the whole of the gallery started clapping. Pongo turned to us and said: *'Noggy, they think you're part of the act too!'* That chap Pongo seemed to think of everything.

6. The dog who could get the laughs

The one thought on our minds as we rose up from our hard seats up in the gods, and made for the exit door, was to get out and get hold of Nelson and get away before they brought the police or something of the sort to us. I suppose it has to do with your upbringing, but it seemed in those days lads were never out of trouble. And so we raced down the stairs without waiting for 'God Save the King', and as we did we could hear the audience still clapping and cheering. It seemed that Blondo had decided to bring the curtain down on that last bow of Nelson's. Perhaps it was because his dogs had been unnerved, or it may have been that after Nelson any other turn would have been an anti-climax.

We imagined old Nelson would be outside waiting for us. But our plan was not to be carried out so easily, for when we went round to the stage door to get Nelson, there was the manager, a man in a dinner suit, and the doorkeeper as well, and they had Nelson behind this sort of half-door.

We were a bit scared, but the manager told us to take it easy, and the next thing Blondo arrived.

'I'm right sorry, mister,' began Noggy.

'Iss this your dog?' asked Blondo, looking down admiringly on Nelson. He was being given sweets and he seemed to have been enjoying himself.

'Yes, mister,' said Noggy. 'An' wait till I get you outside!' Noggy warned Nelson, although he wouldn't have laid a hand on him.

'Don't sspeak like that to thiss vunderful dog,' said Blondo. He was some kind of a foreigner. A Russian or something of that sort, but a very decent geezer. Anyway, a long story short, as they say, Noggy, Pongo and myself left the Grand Theatre with a shilling each in our pockets, and old Nelson not short of sweets, and it was fixed that Blondo would call round at Noggy's next day to discuss Nelson.

Sure enough a taxi-cab drove up our street the next afternoon and stopped at Noggy's door. Folk came to

their doors and watched out of their windows. It wasn't once in a twelvemonth you saw a taxi-cab in our street. Out stepped Blondo. Or at least he must have stepped out because I chanced to be with Noggy, about to go off to toss the pigeons, when he arrived. So being one who always liked to hear what was going on I listened to it all.

For a start, Blondo had an early edition of the local paper, the *Bolton Evening News*. It seems that their critic had been in the Grand Theatre the evening before – and even he had been taken in. He thought Nelson belonged to the act, and he said it was a show not to be missed on any account.

Ranee made Blondo a cup of tea. You always did that the first thing in Bolton when anybody called – you put the kettle on. That is, if you had any decency about you. Homes where they didn't put the kettle on almost at once were not considered much bottle, as the saying went.

Blondo got down to what he had come about – Nelson. He wasn't a rich man but he would pay a fair price. Jud said they didn't think they could sell him. But Blondo insisted:

'Last night,' he said, waving his cup of tea around as he spoke, 'I got a *laugh*! Understand me, a *laugh*! Then I got another *laugh* and another *laugh*. I brought the curtain down on those *laughs*.' The way he said *laugh* you would think it was one of the rarest and most wonderful experiences in life.

'And then it came to me what iss missing in my show – people never laugh. My dogs are wonderful – they are brilliant – they get tremendous appreciation, clapping, applause – but they get no *laughs*.' Then he stooped and patted old Nelson: 'This is the fellow for *laughs* – and now that I have tasted them I must have *laughs*.' He stood up – he kept watching Nelson. In fact Blondo could hardly take his eyes off him. 'How much will you take for him?' he asked, dipping into his inside pocket and taking a fat wallet out.

'It's no use, mister,' said Ranee.

'Why not?' said Blondo.

'No use,' said Jud, 'not if you were to tak' a thousand pound out of your wallet. I daren't sell 'im. It's more than my life's worth.'

'Thiss I do not understand,' said Blondo. 'You need money like everyone else. I will be kind to him. Why not sell him? I will giff a very good price.'

'Because,' said Ranee, '*he's not ours to sell.*'

7. The sailor home from the sea

What Ranee said was absolutely true. And it settled the matter there and then with Blondo, who went away greatly disappointed. Nelson was not their dog. He lived with them, and had lived with them for years, but he was Uncle Gus's dog, and he knew it. Uncle Gus was Ranee's younger brother, and he was a seaman. He had run away from home to join the merchant navy when he was thirteen. And often he would be away for a year at a time, and then home for a week or two. But he could have been away for years – Nelson would have remained faithful to him. That is the extraordinary thing about a good dog – he never forgets who his true master is. And I think I can say that no animal is more faithful than a good dog.

It chanced that the very same week that Nelson had done his turn at the Grand Theatre, we were all sitting at the streetcorner on a weekday evening, Nelson in

amongst us, when suddenly that dog seemed to go on the alert. One moment he was his usual self, the next he had gone quiet and still.

'What's up, Nelson?' I said.

Nelson ignored me. For a second or two he looked as if he was not certain of himself. Then he raised his nose and sniffed the air, as though he had detected the trace of some deeply significant smell.

'I think,' said Noggy, 'he must 'ave smelled Uncle Gus.'

The words *Uncle Gus* had no sooner left Noggy's lips than Nelson made a leap. He knocked Pongo and me over in his excitement. The next thing he went speeding down the street, just skimming past youngsters playing in the gutter, just missing an old woman, and disappearing round the corner, leaving a faint cloud of disturbed dust in the air.

'I'll bet Uncle Gus is on his way home,' said Noggy.

'But how would Nelson know?' asked Pongo.

'Don't ask me,' said Noggy. 'He just knows. In fact he's been funny all day. He definitely knows something.'

'Why don't you go after Nelson?' I said.

'Why should I?' said Noggy. 'He knows but I don't know I'd look a right muggins, wouldn't I, if I ran off to find somebody that wasn't there. But Nelson doesn't mind – he'd run from here to the North Pole to see his master.'

Where Uncle Gus was when Nelson disappeared I do not know, but what I do know is that some ten minutes later who should hove into sight around that same streetcorner but Uncle Gus – everybody called him that – with Nelson in close attendance. And if anyone imagined they had known the real Nelson before they had seen him with Uncle Gus, they would now realize their mistake. He looked a different dog. His tail was

sort of stiffened and stood in the air, half wagging with every step he took, and he had a slight challenging air, as much as to say: If any of you lay a finger on my master, heaven help you!

Uncle Gus was at once a conspicuous figure in our neighbourhood. He was a fairly tall man and lean, and his smiling tanned face was very noticeable amongst people who seemed always pale. He didn't carry a suit-case like ordinary people would be seen with, which in my opinion rather sets one down a bit, but he had a sailor's kitbag or whatever it's called, a sort of round hold-all affair, fastened with two cords, and this was set casually upon a shoulder. Uncle Gus gave the impression of not being even aware of it.

He wore a dark blue jacket that was loose, and had a sailor's jersey with a polo neck, and he moved with a rolling gait. This walk was the most striking thing about him, for around our street everybody had gone to work in the mill at an early age, and learnt to respond to factory buzzers and the like, so it often seemed that they walked like clockwork figures, fast and jerky. If you didn't speed along you would get pushed off the pave-ment. But Uncle Gus moved with a free and easy swing, and a slight roll that came, so they said, from learning to walk on a moving deck. Also, he didn't look downwards, but seemed to gaze ahead, like a man used to gazing long distances.

Noggy jumped to his feet as Uncle Gus approached: 'Uncle Gus!' he said. 'Do my Mum an' Dad know you're home?'

'They will,' remarked Uncle Gus, 'when they see me. Nelson always gives me my welcome.'

Nelson sort of raised his head in a dignified manner and surveyed us boys with a cool stare. You would never have imagined that a short time before he had been in amongst us. Now he was sort of aloof and kept us at a distance. His master was back and his true self could come out. He wasn't going to toady up to small boys any more – well, not whilst Uncle Gus was at home.

'I'll run in an' tell 'em,' said Noggy.

Uncle Gus detained Noggy with an affectionate hand on his shoulder: 'Take it easy, boy,' he said, '– take things as they come. No need to tell 'em. No need to tell anything in this life. In time everything becomes known.' He could be a bit mysterious at times could Uncle Gus. Then he looked at all of us: 'Hy, lads!' he said.

'Hello, Uncle Gus,' I said, and most of the others greeted him the same way. You couldn't have too many uncles, not if they were all like Uncle Gus.

'I expect you lads could do with some fish an' chips,' he said. The nice thing about Uncle Gus was a sort of sea smell, a smell of brine and salt air. It was so fresh.

Nobody raised an objection to fish and chips. 'Is it fish an' chips between us,' asked Noggy, 'or individual?'

'Individual,' said Uncle Gus, 'every time.' And he put his hand in a trouser pocket and pulled out a handful of silver.

'Let me see,' said Noggy, counting us, 'that'll be tuppence for the fish an' tuppence-worth of chips apiece?'

'Did you say *peas*?' said Pongo, always one for getting something extra.

'I said *apiece*!' said Noggy.

'Fish, chips, peas, beans, the lot,' said Uncle Gus, handing Noggy the bright half-crowns. 'Money no object.'

I think that is a beautiful saying. I thought so then and I think so today. But apart from Uncle Gus I've scarcely heard another soul say it. *Money no object*. What it means simply is that there is no shortage of money – so don't give it a thought – just get what you want. A beautiful saying. *Money no object*.

.'Right, lads,' said Uncle Gus, '– have a good time.'

Lots of people use that expression, *Have a good time*, but Uncle Gus was one of the few who backed it with some substance. His words did not simply fly through the air. He wasn't one of those people, of whom one preacher has spoken, who are ready enough to do the Good Samaritan – but without the oil and the twopence. Uncle Gus gave you the money to have a good time with. And as we got ready to dash off to Bibby's fish-and-chip shop, Uncle Gus made his way down the street, rolling along, with Nelson at his heels, rolling along in a somewhat like manner.

8. Dog and master take the air

There was a woman lived in our street, a Miss Peabody, and it was generally allowed that she was a fine upstanding woman. Except, perhaps, when she was down on her knees mopping and stoning the stone flags outside her front door around half past six on a Friday morning before going off to work. She had a hefty b.t.m., as they used to call it, and if I was on my way home after attending the 6.15 a.m. Mass – there was a devotion known as the Nine Fridays – I found it better to walk on the other side of the street altogether. She took up most of the sideset, and you just dare not tread on her clean steps, or she would have flung the rubbingstone at you.

You couldn't call Miss Peabody a beauty, but she was most respectable and had a very good job at the ropewalk. That was the name given to the long low building where they made rope, banding and string. In a way, it must be admitted that in those days a good regular job did seem to enhance a woman's looks, the same as a few pounds in the savings' bank may have improved a man's. She was the foreman – even if it was a woman you called her the foreman – of the twine and banding department.

She wasn't very old – but come to that she wasn't very young either. In fact, she had one of those faces that scarcely ever change. I think this is mostly the case with people who seem to experience very few feelings deeply. It seems there is little or nothing happens underneath to change the face. Her mother had died and now she lived

54

alone and kept a big fat tomcat called Samuel. In a way Miss Peabody had become too posh for our street. Either the street had gone down in the world over the years, or she had gone up in it, or it might have been a bit of both. Let's say that she was inclined to keep herself to herself. Being a foreman she was forced to, for young boys and girls who got work at the ropewalk would take advantage.

One reason I've brought Miss Peabody in to this story is because out of our entire street of people and children who liked and admired Uncle Gus, she was the sole one who appeared not to like him, and in fact to disapprove of him strongly.

When Uncle Gus came home for his break on this occasion he adopted his usual relaxed routine. He wasn't a chap to be up first thing of a morning. He liked to get up later, and enjoy his breakfast in peace, with Nelson up against his chair, waiting for the bits of bacon and sausage and other delicacies Uncle Gus would pass down

to him. I should perhaps add that when Uncle Gus arrived home one of the first things he did was to send Ranee shopping to one of the poshest shops in town. The corner shop wouldn't do for him.

'Get everything of the best, Ran',' he used to say, 'the best tea, the best coffee, the best bread, an' the best bacon an' sausage. No half measures, please – money no object.' And he would press money into her hand . . . even the huge white five-pound note of the time, with its black print and its crispy crackle suggested undreamt-of opulence. I suppose you could afford to talk and act like that if you came on leave once every year or two. He was a very lavish man with his money.

It was summer holidays at the time, and sometimes it came that I would be at Noggy's around half past ten in the morning when Uncle Gus was finishing breakfast. If you are a lad and mostly used to the ways of men and women who are married, you find yourself most appreciative of the entirely different ways of a bachelor. I admired Uncle Gus's easygoing single-man ways. As I say, you get married men, fathers especially, and there's something slightly harassed, impatient, nervous and grumpy in the way they go about things in the morning. But Uncle Gus seemed to radiate peace and serenity.

He was a dog man. It seems odd for a sailor to be a dog man, but that's the way it was. From being a toddler until going away to sea he had always had a dog. And during his stays on shore he had always had a dog. He reckoned he just couldn't have settled down to life at sea without knowing he had a dog at home. Other men had wives or families to think of. He liked to think of his dog. He firmly believed that no home was a home without a dog. And I would say he was near enough right. In most homes in those days people had little samplers displayed on the wall. These were usually framed pieces of embroidery into which some little saying had been woven, the most popular being: '*What is Home without a Mother?*' There was a sampler on the wall in Noggy's home, one specially designed and made for Uncle Gus, and its message read: '*What is Home without a Dog?*'

The funny thing about a dog is that he will always and instantly recognize a true dog man or dog woman. These are persons with a genuine understanding of dogs. They are not soft or sentimental with dogs, but on the other hand they are never unfair or badtempered. They seem to know by instinct that the one thing they need to inspire in a dog – or indeed almost any animal – is a sense of trust. And they know that the one thing a good dog never wishes to do is to upset his owner and so incur displeasure. If he does so, it is nearly always a mistake. So they don't keep punishing animals. They never nag them. One thing an animal can't stand is being nagged at. Nothing makes a horse more nervous than a young girl keep nagging at it, or even keep talking to it. Horses like nice quiet attention. Most dogs like a bit of praise and a bit of fun. People who really understand animals – and they are few – seem to know by instinct what to do. They train them very slowly but surely – until that animal knows what the owner wants very often before the owner himself knows.

Nelson would do what Ranee and Jud told him, and mostly what Noggy told him, too, but nobody had to push him too far. He wouldn't stand for it. He would go off in a huff, as much as to say, I don't know why you lot are lording it over me, do this that and the other! Remember a dog has only one master, and in my case you don't happen to be that master. Yes, old Nelson could be quite uppity at times. But with Uncle Gus the relationship was totally different. It was as though that dog was somehow tuned in to him all the time.

Anyway, after breakfast Uncle Gus would light his briar pipe. He didn't smoke twist or any cheap tobacco, but had a tin of the best tobacco money could buy, and a very good pipe, and when he smoked you got a lovely fragrance round the place, the same as when someone smokes a good cigar. There's nothing beats a nice rich smell around a house. I go for smells more than anything. Then he would put his feet up on another chair and read the newspaper. Nor did he read the paper like a married man does – getting annoyed and making comments. Uncle Gus read the paper as though all the news didn't really matter. 'Take things as they come,' he used to say.

I remember I once remarked now nice it must be to have such a pleasant and easygoing man as Uncle Gus around, and Ranee said: 'Don't forget – he's a single man.'

So I happened to say: 'I wish my Dad were a single man.'

They all looked at me for some reason and Jud said: 'Dusta not realize what that would make thee!'

Noon was the time that suited Uncle Gus best to go off with Nelson for their day out. The streets have got properly aired about that time, he used to say – any earlier and they're that bit damp and musty after the night's been on 'em.

When Uncle Gus went out it seemed that three parts of the atmosphere of Noggy's home went with him. There are people like that, whose presence so comfortably spreads itself about a room that when they go out the place seems horribly empty – and a bit depressing. Mind you, that is not to say that Jud didn't have something about him. He had been a soldier for four years during which there had been the Great War, and any man who has been in a war of that sort cannot help but have some character. What Jud perhaps lacked, which most married men seem to lack, is that nice warm expansive manner of the moneyed man who has no wife or family to keep.

Uncle Gus would be wearing his nice easyfitting seaman's suit and the big jersey, and he had a nice dark seaman's cap, worn rather to the back of his head, his thick curly hair sticking out, and somehow or other he would always manage to have a nice fresh rose in his buttonhole. I don't feel right, he used to say, without my rose or my dog when I'm home. I suppose they represented life ashore.

Yes, Nelson would be there at his side. And I mean at his side – with Nelson's ear rubbing up against Uncle Gus's trousers. It seemed to me that Nelson would suddenly discover he had a chest at these times, for he would strut along with his chest out and tail up and that one eye challenging all it met. Although Nelson and I were the best of pals, he would scarcely recognize me at such times. It wasn't that he snubbed me – in fact now and again he would give me a quick wink – it was more as though he were saying: I'm out with the guv'nor now – d'you mind if I don't speak? I'd rather he didn't know that you and I were on the matey side. A more cunning dog would be hard to find.

Now it seemed that, by some chance, Miss Peabody would be home for dinnertime (*lunch* was what you ate at work about nine o'clock in the morning where we lived). She might even be giving a swift wipe over to her front door or windows, for she was a scrupulously tidy woman. Like as not her blinking tomcat Samuel would be there at the door, sunning himself and sort of challenging all comers. Miss Peabody always gave Uncle Gus a look. I've seen her do it, and I've seen the look, and it wasn't one easy to describe. It was a sort of *'I wish I had you in tow for a day or two – I'd change your ways for you.'*

Of course, Uncle Gus wasn't blind. He sort of got the message. And for a reply he would whisper something to Nelson. It only needed the least whisper. Then Nelson would start letting out the most horrible low growls, like an angry lion with a sore throat. Then Samuel the tomcat would stiffen up, tail all a-wagging at the end, as much as to say: *I'm ready for you.* Then he would let out the most horrendous hiss. Cats are strange creatures. Marvellous creatures in many ways. Dignified and crafty. And very often more than a match for a dog. But if any cat imagined it could intimidate Nelson with his master in attendance it was sorely mistaken. For old Nelson would fasten that one eye on the hissing Samuel. There must be something different about a dog with one eye, something that can't be pinned down, not even by a tomcat, for very soon Samuel would cease hissing, drop his gaze, stop his tail, and pretend there was some urgent matter to be attended to indoors, and slowly and carefully slink inside, avoiding turning his back so far as he could.

Then Uncle Gus would give another whisper, Nelson would stop growling, and perhaps put his head in the air, letting out one of his throaty chuckles. Uncle Gus would grin, and the pair of them would go along as though sharing a good joke. As Miss Peabody turned her gaze on them, it seemed there was malice in those eyes of hers. Spinster women like Miss Peabody don't seem to like single men like Uncle Gus going around without a care in the world. You'd swear she wanted to get her mitts on him – if such an idea had not been unthinkable.

Once away from the streets Uncle Gus could step it out. Actually these easygoing walkers are very deceiving, for they've got their own rhythm, and since they don't tire easily they can cover long distances. Uncle Gus

would set off right over the moorlands, and come out at some little village ten or fifteen miles away.

It is here where I've got to admit of a weakness in old Nelson's character – and perhaps in Uncle Gus's too. After such a long walk Uncle Gus would be thirsty, and so would Nelson. And somehow Uncle Gus wasn't all that crazy on tea, except for breakfast. On a warm afternoon or early evening after a long tramp, what Uncle Gus liked was beer – a nice pint of beer at one of the oldfashioned village pubs. These pubs had little low-ceilinged taprooms or vaults, and the moment you entered all was quiet, like some little dark dell in fairyland, and there were no loud voices, no arguments – all was peace and beer.

Nelson liked to fit in with all Uncle Gus's wishes, and if his master was having beer then he too would have beer. Uncle Gus would order a pint for himself and a half-pint for Nelson, and he would ask for a nice clean dog dish, and pour Nelson's out before he touched his own, and then say *Good Health*, and he would take a good drink at his pint and Nelson would start lapping up his half-pint.

You can nearly always tell when a dog is really enjoying food or drink, for he's got a way of moving his weight from foot to foot, and making further starts, so that he can get it down faster, and yet savour it to the full. That was the way old Nelson used to drink. All very nice in a way, just one half-pint. Ah, but on rare occasions Uncle Gus might have had one or two pints more than he ought to have done. Very sad, very sad indeed, for then Nelson also would have drunk too much. I'm not making light of it – it is a very serious problem. No dog should be allowed much more that a half-pint of beer a day. This is a wellknown fact – or ought to be. It is plenty for any reasonable dog. But Nelson was no heel-tapper as they call it, and so long as Uncle Gus was drinking he would not pack in. Although he couldn't stand his round as they say, he could always drink what was put before him.

9. A man you'll not meet every day

It would not happen very often, of course, this three sheets in the wind caper, and certainly never more than once on any home leave for Uncle Gus. But to be strict, once can be more than enough for that carry-on – as shall later be seen. Normally Uncle Gus and Nelson came home together in the evening about eight o'clock and Uncle Gus would send out for fish and chips for everybody around, including Nelson, of course, who was very partial to cod and chips, and the cats, which preferred plaice. Uncle Gus had travelled the entire world, but swore there were no better fish and chips to be got than at Bibby's at the corner of Birkdale Street.

But on these rare tippling occasions Uncle Gus and Nelson would roll home a little later than usual. Uncle Gus would mostly be singing, and his favourite song was: 'I'm the Man You'll not Meet Every Day'. He had a very pleasant tenor voice, and he was never blurred or slurred like some men are after drinking, nor was he loud or raucous in any way. Let me make it clear – Uncle Gus was never drunk, but might be said to be merry. He sang in a pleasing light manner, as though singing to himself. Nelson, ever faithful, would accompany him by a sort of baying to the moon, which really sounded awful, but no one liked to tell him. 'He's got so many good points,' said Uncle Gus on one occasion, 'so why throw in his face his one weak one.'

Miss Peabody would, of course, be standing at the

door, taking a little fresh air before having her cup of cocoa and biscuit and going to bed. Odd how she seemed always to be there when Uncle Gus was around, but there it was. And it was quite a sight to see the encounter, as it were, between her and Uncle Gus. He was of the oldfashioned kind, Uncle Gus, never disrespectful to a lady – not to anyone in fact – although he might be a bit waggish. He would speak to all the neighbours along the way, slip coins to the youngsters, and continue to sing softly his song: 'I'm the Man You'll not Meet –'

When he came abreast of Miss Peabody he would stop singing and raise his sailor's cap: ''Evenin', ma'am,' he would greet her. Nelson did not exactly go for this sort of flapdoodle (as he may have imagined it to be) and after having had a few drinks he was inclined to be saucy,

and would let out a few threatening growls. And on one occasion he actually cocked a leg up and would have committed an unpardonable offence on Miss Peabody's clean doorstep if Uncle Gus had not chanced to spot him in time. He severely admonished Nelson in front of Miss Peabody.

But Miss Peabody's face at such times – and I watched her more than once – was what is sometimes called a study. It was a study in I don't know how many emotions. You felt she didn't know whether to kick Uncle Gus or kiss him. As I say, he was a very handsome man. And perhaps in a way she envied his free and easy ways. After all, she was a worker, a foreman of course, but she had to regiment herself with numerous disciplines, so as never to be late, and never to stay off work ill, and all that sort of thing. Not an easy life for Miss Peabody. Let us be quite fair to her.

You could almost see the various lumps rising up in her gullet as she looked at Uncle Gus. Those curls jutting out from under his cap seemed to add some devil-may-care look. But, of course, she could not fault Uncle Gus's courtesy, or indeed his gallantry, for he wouldn't just touch his cap, but raise it with a flourish. And always give a slight bow. Uncle Gus was really one of Nature's gentlemen. So that the least Miss Peabody could do was to respond with a stiff movement of her head. One time, when he raised his cap, she looked at him and Nelson, and then remarked: 'Not a very edifying sight I must say!' Somehow that remark did not come off, for it was clear that not only was it something she had read somewhere, but also she must have been practising it, for as they say in the theatre she was rotten perfect in her delivery and there was no life behind her words.

However, another time, she looked at the gallant seaman, and then raised her hands upward and outward, as though inviting him to come into her arms, like one might to a small child. Then she seemed to catch herself on, as they say, and let out a half-stifled sob of some sort and turned and disappeared into the house, slamming the door behind her. Uncle Gus looked rather upset. He was a man of tender feeling.

But perhaps the very happiest part of Uncle Gus's stay was when he was going off to sea again. I know this may sound callous, but we must keep to the truth. He nearly always went off on a Saturday morning, and would be accompanied to Trinity Street station by Noggy, Pongo and myself, and always Nelson. We lads used to argue who could carry Uncle Gus's gear for him.

We always loved to get to the station early. On the way there we would pass the open market, so for a start we would get fruit bought for us – apples and oranges, anything that was going. This was an absolute treat for us, since the most we could afford in the fruit line was a *ha'penny cut apple*, which meant that the stallholder would pick up a rotten apple out of a box at the side, cut off the bad part and let you have the remainder for a halfpenny. It was unknown for a boy to have a go at a full apple except when Uncle Gus was at home. After that we couldn't get to the station quick enough to get going on the chocolate and toffee machines. In went your penny – supplied by the smiling Uncle Gus of course – and out came a bar of chocolate or a little slab of toffee. Nothing so exciting as those old machines on railway platforms, with the steam engines snorting away and adding to the excitement. Meanwhile Uncle Gus would be pacing the platform with Nelson at his side, the pair of them seeming to move in step, and at the same time if you chanced to look at them you would imagine they could be thinking the same thoughts.

Finally, in would steam the Liverpool train. There

would be all the usual excitement of doors opening and people hurrying out. And then Uncle Gus would step aboard in his usual unhurried and unflurried style. As if by magic three single shillings would appear in his palm as he shook hands. One each for Noggy, Pongo and me. We used to pretend to refuse of course. I mean a shilling was a lot of money at the time. But Uncle Gus would have none of it. 'Money no object,' he would say. What a marvellous saying! I wonder why more adults don't take it up. It was not only heart-gladdening, but it was very reassuring. It gave you this feeling that the world was not such a bad place after all. And it seemed to turn your mind to loftier thoughts, for if money was no object you didn't have to be tied down thinking of it all the time. If grown-ups only realized, I used to think, how much a lad appreciates having money spent on him – and being given to him as well. Girls love it, too, I reckon.

Then the guard would blow his warning whistle. And

it was at that moment you would see the difference between a human being and a dog in the nature of their feelings. For Noggy, Pongo and myself would be chewing our toffee, one hand in the pocket to make sure we didn't lose the precious shilling, and at the same time calling out our goodbyes and Godspeeds and all the rest of it, but poor old Nelson would be looking up at his master, who was half-leaning out of the window, and Nelson would be looking up at him with a pitiful sadness.

A minute before, Nelson would be at Uncle Gus's side, not leaving him for a moment. Living in some forlorn hope, it seemed. But once that compartment door was shut that poor dog realized his master was going away again. Even lads like us, lighthearted and irresponsible, could not be unaware of Nelson's misery. Then the departure whistle would sound, the last door or two would be slammed shut, and the engine would let forth its loud commanding chug of steam, and the train would slowly begin to draw out, with Uncle Gus waving to us.

I could hardly bring myself to look at Nelson at such times. In fact I can hardly bring it back to mind without having to hold back a tear or something. That poor dog would stare with disbelief at Uncle Gus as he was slowly being drawn away. *You're not leaving me again are you!* seemed to be what he was saying. *Do come back soon – I do miss you. These other folk are all right – but you are my master.*

Then, when that Liverpool train went slowly round the bend in the line and disappeared from sight, Uncle Gus with it, old Nelson seemed to be frozen to the platform. It was as though some heavy weight had suddenly descended upon him, and it seemed he could not move. He looked so forlorn and grief-stricken. Sometimes the sight of him, watching, watching, watching – as though he would stay on that one spot until his master returned – would kind of upset us. And as much as lads are disinclined to show their tender feelings, it was hard to hide them.

Even old Pongo, who couldn't be called soft-hearted by any means, would say: 'I'll not be a minute – I'll just go for a whats-it.' We knew he was only getting out of the way until he could get his face back to normal. He used to get all funny wrinkles round his eyes when he was upset. Not a bad chap at heart old Pongo. Noggy and myself would then try to start coaxing old Nelson with chocolate. Normally old Nelson was extremely fond of the odd bit of chocolate, and although he wouldn't

take your hand with it as some dogs do, he was never slow to respond. But now he would look at the chocolate as though he didn't know what it was and in any case didn't want it. And he would look at us as much as to say: *If only you knew what I am feeling*.

After a time Nelson would begin to stir. We never liked to hurry him at times like that. 'He'll come back, Nelson,' we'd say. 'Don't take it to heart so.' Then we'd all go along to the platform exit. There was a ticket-collector there who had seen Uncle Gus go off more than once, and I think he summed it all up with the remark as he patted Nelson on the way out: 'Every time he turns up here like a young puppy with his master,' he said, 'but when he goes off without him he looks like a weary old dog.' And it was true. I don't think there is a more feeling animal in this world than a good dog.

10. Old Paleface encounters Jud

Life goes on, as they say, and in time old Nelson would settle in once more – not that he had forgotten or would ever forget his master. There is one thing that drives out unhappiness or at least helps it to be forgotten, more than anything else, and that is *work*.

Ranee and Jud always kept Nelson more or less on the go. And as Noggy used to say, a busy dog is a happy dog. In fact Noggy used to talk about Nelson 'following the gun' – what that meant I didn't know, although I certainly liked the sound of it. Jud used to go about town with the pony and cart, picking up old timber to be used for firewood, and anything else that might be handy. Nelson nearly always went with him, for with the dog guarding the cart and its contents nobody could steal anything.

During the holidays Noggy and myself very often went with him, too. And just to give you some idea of the sort of chap Jud was I'll tell of one simple incident that happened.

They were trying out traffic lights for the very first time in Bolton, at the crossing where St George's Road met Knowsley Street. Up till then they had always used traffic policemen. But these traffic lights had been working more or less on trial for some months.

So along goes Jud with the pony and cart, the cart loaded up, and Nelson on the cart, and Noggy and myself hurrying along on the pavement – for we didn't want to put extra weight on the pony. There was this rise – a little brew we would call it – as Knowsley Street met St George's Road, and when we got to it the lights turned red.

'Gee up! . . . come on, old boy,' Jud encouraged the pony, and went straight across the road with the lights at red against him.

There was a tramcar had to put its noisy brakes on, and a lorry had to slow down and let him pass, and there was a car also had to come to a halt. There was also a big fat police-sergeant watching from behind a lamp standard, and when he saw Jud coming across he ran in front of him.

'Hy you, stop, I say!' yelled the sergeant. 'I want a word with you!'

'Not ruddy likely!' yelled Jud, urging the pony on. 'You don't think I'm stopping a horse on a brew. Outa the way!' And if the sergeant hadn't been nifty on his feet the cart would have been over them. 'Wait till I get round on the flat!' shouted Jud. 'You wait!' roared the police-sergeant.

This police-sergeant weighed about nineteen to twenty stone, and was nicknamed Old Paleface on account of his face being so red. You'd think his fat cheeks were going to burst all over the place at any moment. It was said in those days that you got promoted in the police force by weight. Any constable under fifteen stone didn't have a chance of promotion. They reckoned weight carried authority. And I'm not at all sure they were wrong.

All Old Paleface could do under the circumstances was follow us – Jud, the pony and cart, and Noggy and myself. Jud went up Bath Street and turned into Clarence Street and with a lot of fuss came to a halt. The sergeant arrived looking redder than ever.

'What is it, constable?' said Jud.

'What about them lights?' said Old Paleface, feeling in his top pocket for his notebook. I got the feeling he didn't care very much for being addressed as 'constable' when he was a sergeant.

'What lights?' said Jud.

'*What lights!*' yelled the sergeant.

Nelson started barking fiercely at Old Paleface and growling in between barks.

'He don't like you raising your voice at me,' explained Jud. 'You'll have to talk quieter – if you can. He might go for you.'

Old Paleface was nearly choking with wrath as he spoke: 'The *traffic* lights,' he said in a low ominous tone, at the same time taking a notebook and pencil out of his top pocket. As I say, he had this very big bloated face that was rather frightening. I mean you never know what's going on behind all that flesh.

'The traffic lights . . . ?' said Jud, and he looked absolutely baffled. 'What traffic lights?' He turned to Noggy and me for guidance.

'He means them red, green an' amber lights, what they've stuck up on the corner,' said Noggy, 'what go in an' out to tell you when to go an' stop.'

Jud looked more baffled than ever.

'I'll bet he hasn't ever even seen 'em yet,' said Old Paleface.

'I've got other things on my mind,' said Jud.

'You came through them at red,' said Old Paleface, opening his notebook.

'Whether I saw 'em or not,' said Jud, 'you didn't expect me to stop an 'orse on an 'ill wi' a full load on, all on account of some blinkin' lights!'

'What do you think the lights are for?' said Old Paleface, opening his notebook.

'Listen,' said Jud, 'I didn't spend four years in the trenches to come 'ome to stop an 'orse on an 'ill to let a tramcar come through. I didn't fight to save a country like that! I'm askin' you, mate – would you stop an 'orse on an 'ill?'

That was the way Jud spoke – without proper sense or logic. And he went on repeating himself until Old Paleface could hardly get it down in his notebook. Yet underneath it all was *something*. I've got a feeling that people who make out they're stupid or getting on that way have their own sort of cunning. Anyway, I can't think what it was that made Old Paleface put his notebook and pencil back in his pocket and walk away. What his face must have been like I can't imagine. But from the stiff stubborn appearance of his enormous back, I thought, pity help the next poor chap that goes through those lights at red.

11. The tragedy at the tram stop

It happened that just before Uncle Gus was due home on leave the next time, Nelson had the bad luck to get bitten by a rat. Now a rat bite can be rather dangerous, since it has a way of festering as they used to say. So that when Uncle Gus arrived home he had Nelson down to the vet next day.

It would take more than a rat bite to get Nelson down. Just the same, he and Uncle Gus took it easy for a few days until Nelson was his old self. Then, one lovely summer day, with Nelson fully recovered, they set off on one of their walks. They passed a farm out in the country where old Nelson had quite a frolic with a young dog called Bessy. All this I was to hear of later. Then they called in for a drink at a little country pub known as The Three Bonny Wenches.

The weather being hot and the walk having been fairly long, and old Nelson perhaps not being quite himself yet, and perhaps being short of fluid after his illness, not forgetting his fun and games with Bessy, they tended to drink perhaps a little too much. They left The Three Bonny Wenches in high spirits and set off for the long stroll home. And it was on their way home the tragedy happened.

Apparently Uncle Gus decided that a ride on a tram for the last mile or two would be best for Nelson. As Ranee said to Gus, in later telling him not to be too hard on himself: 'What you did,' she said, 'you did out of kindness.' So they stood waiting for the tram. Uncle Gus and Nelson, master and dog, and old and affectionate friends, each having drunk more than was perhaps good for him, and when the tram came along, a big one with a top deck, Uncle Gus went out into the roadway to meet it.

The driver saw him and there was this noisy clanging of brakes, which trams always made, and the shuddering that accompanied the bringing to a halt the many tons of metal. Now, whether Nelson got it into his head that the tram was going to hit Uncle Gus and he was going to protect his master, or whether Nelson misjudged the distance between himself and the tramcar or not was never known. There was much discussion about the matter

later. But what actually happened was that Nelson went head first into the iron bumper of the tram. Nelson was killed on the spot.

The tram driver and the conductor tried to help, but it was no use. The faithful dog was dead. Uncle Gus took it hard. He took it very hard. And he blamed himself. He didn't cry or anything like that. Although he may have shed many tears inside himself without allowing others to see. Anyway, he got a taxi and brought Nelson home in it.

Terrible was the grief in that home when the dead body was brought in. Jud had got a large wash basket and Nelson was put into it. In fact I saw him in it that very evening. All the lads came from all over the place. Something pathetic about a bunch of young lads standing with their caps off paying their last respects to a dead dog. And now there was the question of burying Nelson. Should it be in the backyard or away up on the hills.

'Gus,' said Jud, 'you leave it to me. That dog did so much for me – I'd like to do something back. I'd like it to be so he was never forgot.'

What Jud did was to take the body to a taxidermist he was friendly with. As everybody knows, a taxidermist is a man who can mount the skins of animals, so that they look absolutely lifelike. They don't normally do dogs, but this chap was a pal of Jud's, and as he said, business was so bad he would have mounted a mouse. 'It 'ad an argument with a tram,' Jud told the man, 'an' the tram won.'

Jud arrived home some days later with Nelson's skin, all mounted and perfect, and it was put up on the wall near the fireplace, in the position of honour. Not that Nelson skinned looked all that handsome. It seems that dogs don't – not like lions and tigers. There is something about a dog, or a cat come to that, which in a way only those who knew him understand. He is not a wild creature. His beauty or character is so often in his nature, not in his appearance. That is not to say Nelson looked awful. Somehow you knew it was Nelson – or what was left of him. But what a dog he had been!

12. Miss Peabody sticks her big nose in

It was a very subdued party that set off to see Uncle Gus to the station on Saturday morning. I know because I was one of them, and I chanced to see the reflection of us all in the window of a second-hand clothes shop called La Bohème, which had a big mirror at the side. There was only one member of that party seemed to sport a self-satisfied grin at the corners of the mouth. I'll tell you who that was later.

People said that Uncle Gus would never recover for many a long day. It seems to have knocked the stuffing out of him, they said. And in a way they were right. For what Uncle Gus did by the way of restitution was to sign the pledge, as they called it, renounce all intoxicating drink. If it can bring about the death of my best friend, Uncle Gus said, I can do without it. And so he did – but the change seemed to make him rather silent. As Jud said, he staggered around blind sober.

There were Noggy, Pongo and myself as usual. And there was this one other person besides Uncle Gus – *Miss Peabody*. Yes, it seems unbelievable, but there it was – *Miss Peabody*! Miss Peabody was the one I fancied I caught with the grin on her mug as I was looking in the shop window. 'Why she has to stick her big nose in, I don't know,' said Pongo. And Noggy said: 'A woman like that would take your own uncle from you.' She had hurried into Noggy's home after the death of Nelson to express her deep sympathy, as she put it. What a wonderful dog it had been, says she who couldn't stand the sight of Nelson. As Jud said, death brings out the hypocrites. Then she had asked Uncle Gus into her place for a cup of cocoa one evening, and she had played him a record, 'Poet and Peasant', on her gramophone that had a big horn. To cheer him up sort of. Pongo's mum had watched it all from the upstairs-front window, which gave you a view straight into Miss Peabody's front kitchen. She reckoned Miss Peabody sat down on the horsehair sofa beside Uncle Gus and took hold of his hand, and that Uncle Gus looked very uncomfortable. All Pongo's family had sharp eyes.

When Saturday came round matters had advanced a little further between them – or so she imagined – so that she took the morning off work and came to see Uncle Gus off. It struck me that one of the odd things in this life is how a person with a lot of push and go can some-how manage to move in and get grips of some sort on someone who is placid and easygoing. I reckon that was what she had done.

No, things were not the same. Uncle Gus had a saying about dogs to the effect of a dog never being critical, never asking questions, and always taking you as you are. But Miss Peabody never stopped asking questions: You won't forget to write, will you? You'll look after yourself, won't you? You'll not forget what I told you, will you? And she had never done straightening his jersey, looking down at his shoes, removing bits of fluff off his coat, and one thing and another. She occupied the poor chap that much that he forgot to give us our coppers for the chocolate machines. Noggy kept pulling back the metal handle of a machine and letting it slam back, just as a reminder. He made a terrific din and got a few black looks from the porters, but it was no use. Miss Peabody sort of masked Uncle Gus from us and kept staring into his face with a right soppy look. No harm in that, I suppose, except it didn't go with her. You knew she was only putting it on.

Then, as the whistle blew, which was always that mar-vellous moment when he slipped us each our shilling, what does Miss Peabody do but get up on her toes and go and kiss him. 'Gussy, darling,' she said. I heard her. So did Pongo. 'That's torn it,' whispered Pongo. 'I'll bet we see no shillings this time.' And how right he proved to be. As for Uncle Gus, the poor chap went red in the face – didn't know where he was for embarrassment. He forgot our shillings all right. He even forgot us. And there was Miss Peabody waving her little hanky and dabbing her eyes for his benefit. Uncle Gus must have taken this one look at her and then buried his face in the far corner of the compartment. The next thing the train

was off. And I can tell you that train was no sooner out of sight than she turned and tripped off quite gaily.

'What a difference,' remarked Pongo, 'between old Peabody an' Nelson. See 'ow she was dabbin' her eyes an' makin' out she was 'eartbroke, an' the next thing she's off like a shot. An' remember old Nelson, how he'd stick there as though glued to the spot – that one eye of his starin' after the train.' Then Pongo added: 'Yon dog 'ad more feelin' than a Christian. But that Peabody dame –' and he said no more, just pulled a face. And when Pongo pulled a face it conjured up all sorts of thoughts.

When we got back and Noggy told Ranee what had happened, she said: 'That one's got 'er eye on poor Gus!' She stood with an iron saucepan in one hand and gazed in front of her, as though seeing into the future: 'Our poor Gussy,' she sighed, '– he's done for. He is that an' all.'

13. The rot sets in

After the death of Nelson it seemed, as Jud put it, the rot set in.

For a start, you couldn't get used to the face of Nelson not being around any more. You caught yourself looking for him or calling him. At the streetcorner he was painfully missed. We had got used to pretending he was a nuisance, and now we realized he had been a blessing. You seemed to miss him at every turn. Especially when you were feeling fed up and unhappy, you missed the way he had of smelling you out and cheering you up.

Tutty Booth seemed to take advantage of Nelson's absence and began to show more of those horrible boring society films and love dramas. There were films with vamps, women with eyes all thick with eye-black and real moony expressions. They were terrible films, yet with no Nelson to set them off the audiences just sort of sat them through. One or two mumbled their complaints. It seems most people need a leader, if it's only a dog.

Around Noggy's home things went from bad to worse. The kids were never in at mealtimes or bedtimes, and there was no one to go off and find them. And if a row broke out there was no one to pacify and quieten things down. The cats now felt they could have the run of the place, and so they began to trespass and so upset the poor pigeons. There's no creature more saucy than a cat who can get away with it. The pigeons got very edgy, and edgy pigeons seem to fall out of love – like edgy people I suppose – and Jud started losing races. Of course the rats began to get out of hand as well. The entire domestic and family atmosphere deteriorated. It wasn't the same home.

It chanced that Uncle Gus had been on a short run and came home rather sooner than usual. He had kept his word and refused to drink any intoxicating liquor. But there was no Nelson for him to go walks with and one could see he was not happy. And of all people, who should attempt to take Nelson's place but Miss Peabody.

'She's all over Uncle Gus,' I heard Ranee say. 'You know what I said – he's done for. You take my word – that man's a goner. You'll be hearin' weddin' bells next.'

And sure enough that was what happened. All in a hurry.

It was painful to see what Miss Peabody had done to Uncle Gus even on the wedding morning. She had been shopping with him a day or two before and now she had got him all togged up in a natty new suit, stiff collar, fancy tie and of all things a bowler hat – or billycock as we called it.

'What a wonderful weddin',' said Jud that evening. 'Everything to drink from weak tea to tap water. An' guess what – she's turned old Gus into a ruddy landlubber! He tells me he's not goin' back to sea – she's cajoled him into takin' a job at the ropewalk workin' under her! Could you believe it!'

'How are the mighty fallen,' said Noggy, who wasn't as illiterate as he made out.

14. The hero in decline

It is a sad thing for a boy to see one of his heroes fade away, as it were, before his very eyes. At least it seemed very sad to me to see the change that came over Uncle Gus once he settled in at the ropewalk.

I had always seen him in his nice loose seaman's clothes, with the cap at the back of his head, and moving along with that nice rolling walk of his. But now, of course, he wore greasy overalls the same as anybody else, and the usual clogs with irons on the wooden soles. The impression one got of the man was somehow different. In next to no time that pleasing seaman's tan disappeared and underneath it seemed that Uncle Gus was as pale as everybody else who worked under a roof. Above all, he lost that nice easygoing swinging gait of the sailor.

I don't suppose he could help that either since Miss Peabody-that-was (she wasn't given her married name of Mrs Glendenning straight off) always seemed to have him in tow, and as she seemed always in a hurry to get back to work Uncle Gus had to hurry alongside her, just that bit behind. The impression she created was that Uncle Gus, having given up his single status, now belonged to her, hook, line and sinker. Just now and again as I passed them, Uncle Gus would give me a funny little wink. I never quite knew what that wink meant, except it seemed to hint – Look what I've blooming sunk to! A right Mary Anne she's making of me!

Now, whether it is that young lads and girls can often see things clearer than their elders I would not like to say, but the fact was that around the neighbourhood the talk was of what a lucky man Uncle Gus was to have married Miss Peabody. I remember one occasion when I was sitting on the doorstep reading *Comic Cuts*, and there were two neighbours, Mrs Brown and Mrs Browitt, supposed to be out sweeping the flags in front of the door but actually gossiping away. As much as I enjoyed reading comics I could never resist listening-in to folk talking, and so I kept my comic in position but cocked my ears at the same time.

'Some folk 'ave all the luck an' don't know it,' said Mrs Browitt. 'Now take that Uncle Gus as they all call him –'

'Ee aye,' said Mrs Brown, 'he fell on 'is feet all right. Got a reg'lar job at the ropewalk an' 'alf the nation out of work.'

'What I say,' said Mrs Browitt, 'he now knows when he's comin' an' goin'.'

''Course he do,' said the other, 'instead of sailin' the Seven Seas in all sorts of weather.'

During this talk it seemed that Mr Browitt had edged his way out-of-doors and thought he'd like to join in: 'Aye, take a stormy night,' he said, 'an' he could be far out in the Pacific, or it could be the Indian Ocean – or say he was walkin' the deck under the skies of the Orient –' I could hardly believe my ears, for it was a well-known fact that Mr Browitt had never even been as far as Blackpool. The story was told of how he had only once been to Southport to see the sea. His son Alec had taken him, and Mr Browitt had sat on a deckchair for nine hours just looking at the sea. And when Alec came back for him and asked him had he enjoyed himself, Mr Browitt had said: 'Aye, it wur all right – but is that all the sea does, just come in an' go out?' And now he was talking about the Indian Ocean and the skies of the Orient as though he knew them all like the palm of his hand. I listened and heard him go on with his tale: 'An' say,' he said, 'there's one of these flyin' fish hits him smack on the chops. Not a nice thing that – to 'ave a flyin' fish smack you one.'

'He's spared all that for ever more,' said Mrs Brown. 'He's safe under his own roof.'

'Excuse me,' said Mrs Browitt, 'under Miss Peabody's roof. She's got her name in the rent book.'

'Aye,' said Mr Browitt, 'with Miss Peabody there beside him.'

And I thought to myself, I'd sooner have a clout from a whale let alone a flying fish than be next to that Miss

Peabody. I may not have mentioned it, but Miss Peabody had a rather hard face. As Jud used to say, it would stand soling and heeling.

'Remember how he used to come swaggerin' home up the street with that dog of his, Nelson,' said Mr Browitt, '– both of 'em a bit tipsy.'

'He's 'appier now,' said Mrs Brown, ''aving his nice cup of cocoa in front the fire with Miss Peabody.'

I couldn't stand any more so I got up and went inside. There was a big and unexpected change coming of which I am eager to tell.

15. The runaway

It might have been that very same evening, or perhaps it was the one after, and I chanced to be in Noggy's playing dominoes with him. He was a fierce domino player was Noggy. His Mum and Dad were talking about Uncle Gus.

'I'm not saying old Gus ain't happy,' said Jud, 'all I'm saying is that he don't look happy. Working at the rope-walk don't suit him,' he went on, 'no more does that Miss Peabody. I can't think why he don't put his foot down.'

'Our Gus,' said Ranee, 'has always been of a gentle nature, ever since he was a baby away in India. Always the quiet one, never one for argument. But don't get the idea in your head that he's a softie. I remember when we came back to England an' my Dad put him working in the mill. Gus came home and said he didn't like it. My Dad said he'd get used to it the same as everybody else. The next day Gus went to work, and the next thing we hear from him is a postcard from Valparaiso – months later. He'd gone off to sea without a word.'

'Where's Valparaiso?' said Jud.

'A seaport in Chile,' said Noggy. 'Bill, your move. Don't keep gawpin'. Get on with the game.'

'The next thing our Gus –' began Ranee, when Jud interrupted her. 'Sh . . . sh . . .' he said, 'I think that's him now.' The door opened and Uncle Gus came in.

To be honest, I could hardly bring myself to look at

him. As I said, he had been my hero. Once he had brought the tang of the sea with him wherever he went, some hint of the vasty deep in that brine smell that clung to his clothes, whilst now he had a bit of a pong of old rope and grease. And he seemed to have gone smaller: '*Who have watched his mould of man, big-boned and hardy-handsome,*' as the poet said, shrinking, I thought, to insignificance, it seemed, under Miss Peabody's constant care and supervision. He can't be all that lucky, I said to myself.

'Cuppa tea, Gus?' said Jud.

'She'll be expectin' me back,' said Gus. 'She makes cocoa. No, thanks.' He still had his nice gentle smile. 'I thought I'd just look in,' he said. He stood there, seeming not knowing what to do or say.

'Come on, Bill,' said Noggy, 'your move.' We were playing for halfpennies – and, as I say, Noggy was a keen domino player. So our game went on.

But I did look up when Uncle Gus was getting ready to go off. I saw him go across to where old Nelson's skin was displayed on the wall. It had become a bit taut over the months, and like Uncle Gus, that too was shrinking. As I have said, a dog skin doesn't seem to keep like lion or tiger skin. It had lost what colour it ever had, what with all the dust, the smoke from the fire and one thing and another, you would never have mistaken it for a leopard skin or anything of that sort. In fact it was becoming tatty.

It seems we don't love such things for their value or their beauty but for what they bring to mind. And it was fairly plain to see on Uncle Gus's face, as he gave an affectionate stroke to that skin, that memories were returning. Memories perhaps of a long friendship, when his dog would always be waiting for him when he came home on shore leave. Memories of walks over the moorlands, and memories of returning, singing together.

I spotted Ranee and Jud watching him also, then Ranee gave Jud a nudge. She didn't say anything, but Jud knew what she meant: Go across and say a nice word or two to the poor chap.

'There'll soon be nothing left of it,' called Ranee.

'There'll soon be nothin' left of any of us,' said Jud. 'Nothin' but dust.'

Uncle Gus nodded, as much as to say: I don't mind how soon it happens to me. As you will have gathered he wasn't a talkative chap.

'Did I tell you I got myself a pure pedigree fox terrier after old Nelson died?' said Jud to Gus.

'Only about two million times you told him,' whispered Noggy aside. 'Come on, Bill – your move.' Between listening-in to the chat and being bullied by Noggy I was losing three-halfpence.

'A beauty,' went on Jud to Gus, 'a real class terrier. Short back, long neck, short ears, thick coat, black an' white, more white nor black – a real champion. And he wasn't a blind bit of use. Couldn't catch a rat – scared of the cats. I had to take him back.'

'You couldn't blame the dog,' said Ranee. 'He was a show dog – not a family and ratter dog.'

'Nelson,' said Uncle Gus, 'was an exceptional dog.'

'He was for sure,' said Jud. 'And to think I took you for granted, old boy.' He patted the skin and a bit fell off. He turned to Uncle Gus. 'Gus,' he said, 'why don't you get yourself another dog?'

'I wanted to. But she won't let me have one,' said Uncle Gus. 'She says they're not hygienic.'

'Hygienic!' snorted Jud. 'A good dog is the most hygienic creature you can find. I'll tell you one thing, Gus, you're lettin' her dictate to you too much – an' I'll tell you another,' went on Jud, pointing a finger at Nelson's skin, 'he wouldn't 'ave stood for it. Not Nelson. He was an obedient dog, but he 'ad some spirit. If you pushed him too hard old Nelson would rebel.'

I don't know whether there was a smut of coal dust from the open fire got in Uncle Gus's eye, or what it was, but I saw him wipe his hand across his eye and he declared: 'An' by gum I won't stand for it!'

Everyone looked at Uncle Gus. It was so unlike him to use such a tone of voice. Even Noggy, who seldom lifted his eyes from his dominoes when he was playing, gave him a look of curiosity.

'Ranee,' said Uncle Gus, and his face seemed to indicate he had taken some quiet decision, 'have you still got my old togs – you know, that I left here?'

'You mean your seaman's gear?' said Ranee. 'Yes, I

have. Every single stitch. Down to your Seaman's Union card. All upstairs in the back bedroom. I washed your jersey so the moths wouldn't get in. Why?'

'Like me to fetch 'em down?' said Jud.

'No, thanks,' said Gus. 'I'll go up. I know my way around.' He hesitated for a moment, took one more look at Nelson on the wall, seemed to square his shoulders in a determined way, and then went through the middle kitchen door and went upstairs.

'I wonder what's come over your Gus?' said Jud.

'It was when you brought up Nelson,' said Ranee. 'Did you see the look in his eye?'

'He's got *something* on his mind,' said Jud.

'He has for sure,' said Ranee.

'Your move,' said Noggy, rather sharply. He couldn't bear to be held back at all, even when playing dominoes he had to be on the go. 'Can't you go?' he asked.

'I can go,' I said. 'I'm just weighin' up the situation.'

'I think I know another chap who can go as well,' remarked Jud. 'And I'd say that he's already weighed up the situation.'

I played my domino. Noggy played his domino. Then I played my next one. Then Noggy went again. Then I was knocking. And Noggy won. So I gave him another halfpenny. I was in danger of going broke.

Uncle Gus suddenly appeared round the kitchen door. There was such a transformation in him that for one moment I thought I was seeing things. He had taken off all his other clothes and was now dressed in his seaman's uniform, all looking nice and loose – looser than ever in fact, for Uncle Gus had lost some weight. In his hand he carried his seaman's cap.

'What's up?' said Jud. 'Tryin' 'em on for size?'

'I think I've seen the light,' said Gus. 'Don't say anything – let me get off first.'

Even Noggy seemed to look up and take his mind off the game for the moment.

'Get off where?' said Ranee.

'I must get back to the sea again,' said Gus.

If you only knew it, Uncle Gus, I thought, you're almost in with a poem. *I must go down to the seas again, to the vagrant gypsy life, To the gull's way and the whale's way where the wind's like a whetted knife.*

There seemed to come to the little room one of those very quiet moments, one of those when it seems everyone is thinking his own thoughts, and these thoughts seem to make a sort of silent sound in one's ear. I wish he'd take me with him, I thought, and the other verse of the poem came to me: *And all I ask is a merry yarn from a laughing fellow-rover, And quiet sleep and a sweet dream when the long trick's over.*

'You don't mean you're goin' off tonight!' said Jud.

'This minute,' said Gus.

'But what'll *she* say when you tell her?' said Jud, beckoning his thumb in the direction of Miss Peabody-that-was's home.

'I'm not going to tell her,' said Gus. 'Goodbye, Ranee,' he said.

'But it don't seem right, Gus,' said Ranee, 'going off like that – without sayin' a word to her.'

'It's not right,' agreed Gus. 'In fact it's very wrong, and may God forgive me.'

'Then why don't you just slip in an' tell her?' said Ranee.

'Because,' said Noggy, 'it's more than Uncle Gus's life is worth. Your move, Bill.'

'The lad's right,' said Uncle Gus. 'You know me, Ranee, I'm a peaceful chap by nature.'

'Aye, you always have been,' said Ranee. 'I suppose it's the only way left to you. But it's a terribly sudden decision.'

'Let's say it's been brewin' for some time,' said Jud. 'Eh, Gus?'

'I suppose so,' said Gus.

Then Gus and Ranee kissed, and Gus came round and shook hands with everyone – even me.

'You won't say a word!' put in Jud to me.

'I can trust Billy,' said Gus. He was not a chap to ask for promises. Then he turned to Ranee. 'I'll write to her,' he said, 'the minute I reach a foreign port.'

'Aye,' said Jud, 'when she can no longer lay her mitts on you.'

'You'll need some money,' said Ranee. 'Where's my purse?'

Uncle Gus put his hand up. 'No, Ranee, I'd rather not,' he said. 'Thanks very much all the same. I've got a shilling or two in my pocket. And I prefer to take things as they come. My name's good in ports all over the world.' Then he added: 'Money's no object.' I seem to hear his voice as I write: *My name's good in ports all over the world.* What a splendid thing to be able to say – *My name's good!* As for *Money's no object*, I've said what I think of that.

I can hardly describe my own feelings at the time – not that I had much chance to indulge feelings the way Noggy kept telling me it was my move. And on top of it I was losing all my ha'pennies. But the fact was, seeing Uncle Gus back once more in his sailor's garb, around which there seemed to linger faint traces of salty sea air, and feeling something of his old spirit, there was reviving in me that feeling of his being a hero of mine. A lad loves to have a hero. Somehow I didn't mind losing the odd halfpenny.

'Take care of yourself, Uncle Gus,' called Noggy, and then added: 'I say, your move, Bill. Don't let the talk stop the game.'

I played my domino, making it *ones* up, knowing Noggy had no ones. That'll keep him quiet, I thought.

'I think I'll go out the back way, if you don't mind,' said Uncle Gus. 'Although I don't like doing it.'

'Aye, nobody'll see you that way,' said Jud. 'An' it's already dark.'

'Are you sure you'll be all right?' asked Ranee.

'Right as rain,' said Gus with a smile. The way he said it I suddenly realized that rain is all right. Rain is wonderful. Right as rain, he said. I saw him make to the back door. It was unbelievable – his old seaman's swinging walk had already come back to him. At the door he decided to turn back, and he came into the front kitchen again, went over to old Nelson hanging on the wall and gave him a pat. 'So long, old mate,' he said.

Then he paused before going off, as a thought suddenly struck him. 'Jud, you know Top o' the Fold farm – y'know over –'

'I know,' said Jud, 'Pendlebury's place.'

What's he bringing up a farm for at a time like this, I wondered. 'It just struck me,' said Uncle Gus, 'there's a young dog up there, Bessy, a bitch – real lively – took a strong fancy to Nelson on our last outing. A very strong fancy.'

'Aye . . .' said Jud, '– what about it?'

'He means there might've been puppies, you big mawp,' said Ranee.

'That's it,' said Uncle Gus. 'If you get one of Nelson's pups you won't be far out. God bless you all.'

'I've got no *ones*,' said Noggy.

'Then *knock*,' I said.

'I have been,' he said. He hated knocking.

'Musta been with a sponge,' I said.

I didn't play my domino. I watched Uncle Gus go off into the night, with these subdued whispers of *Godspeed* and *God bless* from Ranee and Jud. Then I looked across at Nelson. For a moment I could have sworn that one eye gave a big wink.

Then I picked out my *double-one* domino and put it down. 'Can you go now?' I said to Noggy, thinking to myself, I can be just as awkward as you!

16. Life goes on

In a way there's not much more to tell. Although I do like to tie the ends up, and perhaps I ought.

Well, I kept on playing dominoes with Noggy, and I've got to be honest about it, I lost all my money – threepence in all – and began to go in debt to Noggy. He knew I always paid up. And I had a feeling it would be worth it. And it was.

About twenty minutes later there was a firm knock on the door and the door half opened. That's what you did in our street unless you were a stranger – you didn't stand on dignity, you knocked, then to save any trouble you half opened the door and called in. You weren't supposed to put your head in and look around in case you saw something you weren't supposed to see. We were very proper.

'Hy, you!' I heard Miss Peabody's voice, sounding not too pleased, 'have you seen the time! Your cocoa's goin' cold – an' Samuel wants to get to bed.'

Jud put his fingers to his lips for us all to be quiet Then he put on a smarmy sort of voice: 'Is that you, Miss P . . . Mrs Glendenning?' he called out. 'Aren't you comin' in?' And he went and opened the door fully.

Miss Peabody now looked in with curiosity. Or what I took to be curiosity. She had obviously been addressing herself to her husband, Uncle Gus, who was missing. I was making out I was looking down at my dominoes, but in fact I was squinting at her out of the corner of my

eye. I don't think she had ever been addressed as Mrs Glendenning before.

'Sixes up,' said Noggy.

'Where is he?' she said.

'Who?' said Jud.

'My husband,' she said.

'You mean our Gus?' said Ranee.

'Who else!' said Miss Peabody. (I suppose by rights I should call her Mrs Glendenning – but I can't bring myself to.) 'My husband.'

'Is he not back yet?' said Jud.

'I wouldn't have come out looking for him if he hadda been, would I?' said Miss Peabody. She was inclined to be sharpish even in someone else's home. Not considered good manners.

'I don't suppose you would,' said Ranee. 'He went off,' she added.

'*Off!* – off where?' said Miss Peabody.

'Now you're askin',' said Ranee.

'I'll *off* him,' said Miss Peabody. 'How long back?'

'Oh quarter of an hour or more,' said Jud. 'Maybe he's taken a walk.'

Miss Peabody looked round the house. Whether she suddenly felt some premonition or what I don't know – but her expression changed. For a moment she had quite a helpless look. I felt sorry for her. She sort of stared at me. I don't know why. Women like Miss Peabody have always had a habit of staring at me. I gave her a look back but I could see she wasn't quite satisfied. 'Funny,' she said, and she went off without even saying goodnight.

'I said *your move*,' said Noggy.

The next morning there was a rumour all over the place that Uncle Gus had gone missing. That same evening the rumour had become a certainty – Uncle Gus had done a bunk. I chanced to pass Miss Peabody on her way home from work, and she gave me another of her piercing looks, as much as to say – You know more than you're making out you know.

Of course, if anyone imagined she was going to collapse and die of a broken heart he would be mistaken. In fact, she seemed to blossom, if you could call it that. Uncle Gus was as good as his word and sent her a postcard from the port of Sydney, Australia. Some months later that was, of course. And being a gentleman he used to send her a regular allowance of money. Not that she needed it, for she was promoted to supervisor and then chief of the twine and banding department. She insisted on being given her proper title of Mrs Glendenning, and for some daft reason that seemed to impress people. 'My husband,' she used to say, 'is on the Australia run. Doesn't get home often.'

But the best thing that came from the happening was that Jud went up to Top o' the Fold farm and came home with a young dog. He was old Nelson to a T, except he had two eyes instead of one. Jud had explained the situation to the farmer, and farmers are not as hardhearted as some people make out – he let Jud go off with one of the litter of three. They decided he could not be called Nelson – only one dog could have that name – but they settled for Horatio instead. Rather a long name, perhaps, for a dog. But there was an Horatio Nelson. And Horatio lived up to his name.

In next to no time the rats had disappeared and the cats were brought to order and the pigeons felt content, fell in love again and started winning races. And to Noggy's home it seemed that peace and good feeling returned once more. But no matter how tattered that skin of Nelson's became there on the wall they would not take it down.

'Without old Nelson,' Jud used to say, 'I doubt if we could have had such a home and family.' I am certain that without him I should have had no story to tell. Many nights in bed I seem to lie awake and recall those old days of my boyhood at the streetcorner – and never do they come back without a very clear memory of old Nelson, in amongst the lads, listening to tales.

Goodnight, everybody!

Two other Puffins by Bill Naughton

MY PAL SPADGER

'Spadger wasn't a big lad, he was on the small side in fact, more wiry than anything, but . . . he had this face that looked somehow different . . . there was something about Spadger, something that bit different, that made him either do odd things or come out with funny remarks.'

Spadger and Bill (who tells the story) grew up together in a Lancashire mining town in the early twenties. They leave school together to start work in mill and mine, but fate does not mean them to work together . . .

THE GOALKEEPER'S REVENGE AND OTHER STORIES

'It was custom for lads to gather at the street corner on summer evenings and discuss trolleying. Spit Nolan was the champion trolley-rider. He had very good balance, sharp wits and he was brave.'

The dramatic story of Spit Nolan is one of thirteen in this collection of funny and stirring tales set in the 1930s. With warmth and vigour it describes the good-humoured exploits of a lively group of boys, and makes entertaining reading.

We hope you have enjoyed this book.
There are more than 1,000 other
Puffins to choose from – some of them
are described on the following pages.

TRAVELLER

Anne de Roo

Lost in a foreign land and miles from civilization, young Tom Farrell is convinced that he won't live to tell the tale. But then he stumbles across Traveller, a remarkable sheep-dog who saves his life and becomes his devoted companion. Set in the 1850s and based on a true incident, *Traveller* is a stirring story of the hardships suffered by the first settlers in New Zealand, and of the enduring loyalty between man and dog.

LASSIE COME-HOME

Eric Knight

Lassie, the prize dog of a cottager's household, is sold to a wealthy family when hard times befall her owners. Taken hundreds of miles away, she does what many collies have done before her, she starts for home so that she can be faithful to a duty – that of meeting a boy by a school-house gate. This classic dog story, which was made into a famous film, and also gave rise to numerous later films and television dramas, is available now for the first time in paperback.

THE NIPPER
Catherine Cookson

Set in the early 1800s in the mining area of north-east England, this is a story of tough people in hard times, a story of sweated labour in squalid conditions. But most of all it is the story of a sixteen-year-old boy's love for a runt pony when his personal world collapses and the green fields are exchanged for a life in the bowels of the earth.

THE MIDNIGHT FOX
Betsy Byars

Tom had hated the idea of going to his uncle's farm for a holiday, but one day he sees a fox jump into the wind-blown grass and each day afterwards he goes out looking for her. He even finds out where her den is, and watches her cub at play. Fourteen times Tom sees the fox, and makes fourteen secret notches on his suitcase, but the fifteenth notch is on the dreadful day when Uncle Fred determines to shoot her for attacking a turkey . . .

THE OTTERS' TALE
Gavin Maxwell

For more than ten years Gavin Maxwell lived with his otter companions in a house at the edge of the sea in a wild and lonely part of the Scottish Highlands. This is the enchanting true story of his life with them and it is illustrated with photographs taken by the author.

JOE AND THE GLADIATOR
Catherine Cookson

Life isn't easy for Joe. At home there is trouble between his parents and at the Tyneside shipyard where he works he has to cope with a nasty bully. But one day he meets an old rag-and-bone man and gets to know his gaunt, intelligent horse, the Gladiator. And what starts as casual interest soon turns into a major test of Joe's courage and determination.

Heard about the Puffin Club?

. . . it's a way of finding out more about Puffin books and authors, of winning prizes (in competitions), sharing jokes, a secret code, and perhaps seeing your name in print! When you join you get a copy of our magazine, *Puffin Post*, sent to you four times a year, a badge and a membership book.

For details of subscription and an application form, send a stamped addressed envelope to:

The Puffin Club Dept A
Penguin Books Limited
Bath Road
Harmondsworth
Middlesex UB7 0DA

and if you live in Australia, please write to:

The Australian Puffin Club
Penguin Books Australia Limited
P.O. Box 257
Ringwood
Victoria 3134